MOHSEN EL-GUINDY

Brothers Khan © 2020 Dr. Mohsen El-Guindy

3rd Edition

ISBN:
Paperback   978-1-953048-97-4

Writers' Branding
1800-608-6550
www.writersbranding.com
orders@writersbranding.com

CONTENTS

DEDICATION

I dedicate this novel to Sharukh Khan, the only actor who was able to make my stubborn tears run down my face.

PROLOGUE

I like movies. I have been watching movies since the early 1950s till now. I have watched American greatest films of all time. Throughout the years I acquired an examining eye that could distinguish a good movie from a bad one.

I became acquainted with camera placement, movement, composition and how adeptly the movie gets from shot to shot, and how the movie would go flat if the director doesn't know how to convey information and emotion through composition and cutting. It became easy for me to detect positive things or negative things about the films i.e. setting, techniques, effects used, and music, etc.

In the 1960s when I was in my twenties, I used to watch some Indian films in which Amitab Bachchan played the leading role. Those films were merely commercial and my opinion at that time was that the Indian film was still primitive and needed further development.

Since that time and till 2015 I haven't watched Indian films. One of my relatives however, was having dinner with us and after a short while she excused herself saying, "If you may excuse me I have an Indian TV episode to watch. " "Oh! Are you serious? Do you find it so important to leave this superb meal in order to watch Indian TV episodes or even an Indian film?" I said amazed. She said, "Come and watch."

So we sat together in the living room watching Indian episodes called Benhayoun Nada. I must say that regardless of some unnecessary elongations, I was fascinated by the performance of Jennifer Singh Grover.

Later, I also watched the Indian TV episodes Iss Pyaar Ko Kya Naam Doon played by Barun Sobti and Sanaya Irani. Regardless of some exaggerations and also some unnecessary elongations, I loved their performance.

Thereafter, I watched the series Ek Duje Ke Vaaste, and I was thrilled to see the outstanding performance of Nikita Dutta. This beautiful young lady is going to have a bright future in the Indian cinema.

Then I started watching the films of the great Indian stars like Sharukh Khan, Ameer Khan, Salman Khan, Seif Ali Khan, the genius Ranbeer Kapoor, the dynamic, Ranveer Singh, the great dancer and performer Hrithik Roshan, the handsome Arjun Rampal and several others.

Talking about the Indian actresses, I watched films for the iconic actresses Mahudri Dixit, Ashwaria Rai, Deepika Padukone, Priyanka Chopra, and the Queen of Bollywood Karina Kapoor.

I must say that these actors and actresses whom I didn't know their names until quite recently have substantially entertained me.

I was also overwhelmed by the work of the romance director Yash Chopra and his son Ditya Chopra as well as the work of Karan Gohar, Rohit Shetty and Farah Khan.

These actors, actresses and directors have made India proud abroad. Bollywood has gone global and the Indian films have been seen in top ten lists of movies in the UK and USA. Although I was immensely entertained by the acting of the iconic stars I have just mentioned, my highly spiritual and emotional heart remained intact of any real influence.

They call Sharukh Khan the king of Bollywood. I said to myself why do they call him that? Is he cleverer than his colleagues in acting, dancing and singing? Does he have a trait that distinguishes him from all others?

In order to know the reason for such denomination - the king - I had to study him further and go deeper into his work. So I watched Sharukh Kan's films with Kajool (Kush Kush Hota Hai; Dilwale; My name is Khan I am no terrorist); With Katrine Kaif (Jab Tak Jaan); With Preity Zinta (Veer Zaara); with Irfan Khan (Billu); with Deepika Padukone (Om Shanti Om and Chenmai Express); with Anushca Sharma (Jab Tak Hai Jaan and Rab Ne Bana Di Jode).

Technically, I realized that Sharuhk Khan was an outstanding actor. He lets his mind concentrate on the aspects of the character, and lets nothing else enter his mind. He keeps all brain waves focused. He is able to easily establish physical and mental transmigration and concentrate solely on the character. He can take you so easily to the world and character he was transmigrating.

But what's so strange about that? Over 50 years I have watched great actors doing what Sharukh Khan was doing and even better! Is he greater than Sir Laurence Olivier, Charles Laughton, Charle boyer, Maurice Chevalier, James Stewart, Robert Tailor, Humphrey Bogart, Henry Fonda, Clark Gable, Spencer Tracy, Cary Grant, Glenn Ford, Gregory Peck, Charlton Heston, Steve McQueen, Rock Hudson, William Holden, Paul Newman, Rod Taylor and so many others? I think not.

Nonetheless, none of these great actors was able to influence me to the extent of shedding tears, but Sharukh Khan was the only actor who was able to make my tears run down my face!

It was in the film "Veer – Zaara" that my heart was crushed when the judge in the court asked Sharukh Khan if he wants to say a few lines during his trial.

Tears welled up in my eyes as I watched him saying: "I, prisoner number 786, look outside through these bars of my prison cell. See the days, months, years turn into decades. From this earth, I can smell the fragrance of my father's fields. This sunlight makes me remember my mother's chilled lassi. This rainfall brings to me the movement of the swings during monsoon. This winter brings me back the memories of the fire on the Lodi night. They tell me that this is not your country. Then why does it seem like mine? They tell me that I am not like them. Then why do they seem like me? I, prisoner number 786, look outside through these bars of my prison cell. I see an angel who has just stepped down from the village of dreams. She calls herself Saamiya and calls me Veer. She is a complete stranger but she fights with me as if she knows me for too long. Listening to her true words, I feel like living again. Listening to her promises, I feel like doing something worthy. They tell me that she is no one to you. Then why does she fight the world for me. They tell me that I am not like her, then why does she seem like me? I, prisoner number 786, look outside through these bars of my prison cell."

Sharukh Khan said these words in a way that touched my heart deeply and I found myself weeping silently.

It was in the film "Billu" that I found myself crying again. On his last day in the village, Sharukh Khan spoke at a local school. He told the children about his own impoverished childhood when he had nothing but a special bond of friendship with another young boy, named Billu. It was Billu who had taken care of him and eventually helped him travel to Mumbai City by giving him his gold earring where Sharukh Khan became a star.

The words of loyalty and gratefulness spoken by Sharukh Khan were so sincere that again I couldn't hold my tears.

I realized then that the trait distinguishing Sharukh Khan from all other actors, was a very special trait that no one else could acquire it but him. God had blessed him with a divine gift – the ability to penetrate into the hearts of people so easily, so sincerely, and so wonderfully. I must say that Sharukh Khan has carved out his niche inside my heart. I simply loved the man.

As far as I am concerned and according to my strict parameters, Sharukh Khan has successfully passed the test. He subdued my obstinate heart and made it surrender to his miraculous performance.

I want to reward him for the beauty he added to my life. I want to present him a gift, but what to present him and he has everything he could possibly wish for.

As a novelist I decided to honor him by writing a story dedicated to him. A story derived from the Indian environment, culture and tradition. The key players in the novel would be Sharukh Khan himself and some Indian actors and actresses I am fond of. This is why I named the co-players with Sharukh Khan in the novel: Salman, Fawad, Mahudri, Ashwaria and Sonam. As for the father of the girls whom I called in the novel 'Misra Bhandari', the magnificent Rishi Kapoor was always in my mind while writing this role.

Well ladies and gentlemen, this is how the novel "Brothers Khan" came to light. A novel I wrote especially for Sharukh Khan, a novel inspired by him and dedicated to him.

CHAPTER 1

There was, in olden time, and ancient age in the land of the Punjab a widowed wealthy man called Misra Bhandari living in his two hundred acre farm. Misra was of a noblest origin. His fathers and grandfathers were the most distinguished of the land.

Misra lived in a large house with his daughters Mahudri, Ashwaria, and Sonam. The mother died while delivering her last child, Sonam. The girls were raised by their governess Asha.

Misra's daughters were of surprising beauty and loveliness, surpassing in elegance and in every grace, endowed with abundant sense, and eminent polite accomplishments. The girls were classy and fabulous.

The farm was run by a farmer called Abed Khan. Abed Khan was poor but was loyal and smart enough that Misra took him into his confidence. Abed was clever in planning, organizing and managing the activities of the farm. Misra showed his gratitude to Abed by granting him a small piece of land to cultivate and benefit from its crops.

Abed lived with his wife and his three sons Sahru, Salman and Fawad in a nearby village. They all lived in a small mud-brick cottage. The boys assisted their mother in household tasks.

There was a vicious outlawed brigand named Agni. He had a brother named Ramesh. With their viciously and blood thirsty gang, they ambushed and robbed people in forests and mountains. They used their power tyrannically and killed and caused ruins almost everywhere.

Agni and Ramesh with their gang raided villages, and captured men, women and children and sold them to wicked plantation owners. Slavery was the source of Agni and Ramesh's wealth. The more land farm owners accrued, the more slaves they needed to work in their plantations. Thus, Agni and Ramesh's profits swelled by income generated from selling slaves to rich farm owners on seasonal basis.

Abed frequently left his wife and boys alone in the cottage, he wished that his boys learn how to defend themselves, their mother and the cottage while he was absent in the farm. Abed had a brother who was master in Indian martial art. Big families of the village hired him to teach their children how to defend themselves against bullying. When the boys had reached the adolescent stage of life, Abed handed them over to his brother to teach them the arts of war.

The boys at a very young age learned from their uncle how to defend themselves when physically attacked. Their uncle taught them that it is not fair to start a fight, but being peaceful does not mean being a doormat. The boys became skillful in combat-wrestling, archery and all kinds of armed combat. They excelled at sword, dragger, spear and axe. In addition to that, Fawad became an excellent archer. The brothers loved what they were trained for and practiced their deadly arts on daily basis.

The boys were well built – tall, large and strong. Sharu, the big brother, was wise and had the sagacity to weigh things exactly. He had a combination of gentleness and hardness. He was compassionate and loving but still firm enough to point the right direction.

Salman was huge and heavy muscled. He relied on his overwhelming strength rather than his head. If provoked he exploded, and did stupid things. Yet, his strength would also cause him trouble, especially when he experienced one of his sudden and extremely frightening outbursts of rage that could have tragic consequences to those who happened to be near him. Though after the rage had passed, his big heart takes him back to his senses.

A wild longing for strong emotions and sensations seethed in Fawad. He was a formidable singer; his songs were simply wonderful, and charming to the senses. His songs gave delicate ecstasy to the listeners.

During the various seasonal operations, Abed took the boys to the farm to help in the plowing and planting, irrigating and harvest.

The Misra farm had been brought to its profitable state by the good management of Abed and his sons and the help of the farmers. The farm produced abundant crops and the market needed more crops.

Each season after harvest, four big wagons pulled by horses were loaded with crops for market. The fattened cattle destined for marketing were gathered and herded by farmers. Abed usually drove one of the wagons, and reliable farmers drove the others. The market was 12 miles away, and the trip usually took a whole day over a rugged road. Abed honestly delivered all the money resulting from selling the crops and cattle to Misra, the landlord.

Abed's boys loved to accompany their father to the distant market and considered the trip fatigue as a fascinating adventure.

Years passed, the seasons came and went and the farm prospered more. In fact, the farm was now making more money than ever.

It was a momentous day when Abed started the seasonal voyage to the market. The crops were placed in four huge wagons pulled by horses. Cattle for sale in the market were gathered and herded to march alongside the wagons. The road was rugged and slow, but the convoy managed to reach the market safely. The crops and cattle were all sold on the market at a fair price.

On its way back to the farm however, the wagons were attacked by bandits from all sides. The outlawed brigands Agni and Ramesh led their gang in a charge against the wagons. Spears and arrows fell upon the wagons. The wagons drivers fled for their lives. Four farmers fell dead, others were severely wounded. The bandits rode alongside the wagons carrying blazing torches. They began to set fire to the wagons, and the flames engulfed the farmers who fled from the fire in panic. The bandits were waiting for them, and they were charged down and slaughtered one by one. It was utter carnage, a sickening slaughter.

When the bandits killed the defenseless farmers, they turned their attention to Abed and his sons. Yet outnumbered and taken by surprise, Abed and his young sons fought with valor and obstinacy. The arrows of Fawad hissed through the dusty air and tore deep into the bandits. The arrows sank to their marks in heart and breast, in brow and brain. Sharu and Salman with their swords and daggers slew ruthlessly without mercy until the earth was a trampled crimson slime.

Abed and his sons realized that without extra help, they stood little chance of resisting the bandit onslaught. They were the only ones fighting now. All the farmers were either killed or cowered, kneeling in the trampled dust.

Abed and his sons kept fighting until the end. Abed sang while fighting with his sword:

> No retreat, no surrender.
> When things go wrong as they sometimes will
> stick to the fight when you're hardest hit.
> It's when things go wrong that you mustn't quit.
> No retreat, no surrender

But Abed and his sons were outnumbered and numbers prevail against courage. Abed's son were now far apart from each other each busy fighting his opponent. Agni was able to single out Abed and stabbed him in the stomach with a hunting knife. Abed screamed and tried to fight back but Agni quickly stabbed him again, then again. Abed fell heavily to the ground sunk in his blood.

Seeing the heavy causalities his gang suffered, Agni and Ramesh ordered their bandits to retreat and station on a hill close by.

The boys seeing their father stretched on the ground sunk in blood, ran to him to give help. But the wound was deep and there was no hope for their father to survive.

With tears overflowing, Sharu lifted his father's head from the ground and put it in his lap. Salman and Fawad wept bitterly seeing their father dying. In a very low and weak voice Abed said before he breathed his last: "Sharu, the money from selling the crops and cattle are in a purse in my pocket. Take the money and give it to the master. Cultivate the land and take care of your mother and brothers."

The boys looked at Agni and his gang on the hill. Sharu shouted at Agni with rage: "I am Sharu Khan the son of Abed Khan the man you killed. One day the Lord will deliver you into my hands, and I'll strike you down and cut off your head."

"And I will eat your heart and drink your blood." Salman shouted with rage."

"And my arrow will pierce your eye." Fawad roared.
Agni was surprised to see that three young boys were able to inflict the most casualties in one day. His gang had suffered 15 fatalities and ten persons had been severely wounded; and as it seemed, the boys were still willing to fight. They were not afraid of him. They are even threatening him with death. He will inquire about these boys. Where they live and what they do?

It's better to retreat now and prepare for another encounter that would eliminate any resistance to his authority in the region. Agni gave order to his gang to retreat to their home city in the mountains.

The three boys prepared from the branches of the trees a stretcher and carried their father to the farm. When they reached the farm, they placed the stretcher on the ground and Misra came quickly to hold Abed and weep ardently on his chest.

"Abed my beloved, the honest, the truthful. Abed my right arm, what happened to you? What am I supposed to do without you? Who is going to manage the things you used to do? Why you left me alone in this treacherous world? Never will I find another like you, you have proved yourself worthy of my trust."

Misra pointed out across the fields to a small hill and said to the boys: "We will bury him up there in the tombs of my family where I will be buried too."

Abed's wife came quickly to the farm to attend her husband's funeral. She was a strong woman and bravely accepted the calamity. She refused to express grief by wailing, beating the chest and cheeks or tearing her closes as ignorant women do. She mourned and wept her husband in silence.

After the funeral, the mother demanded to see Misra the landlord. Misra was happy to see her. The mother took her children with her. They all met in the guest room. Misra's daughters were all present, busy sewing, knitting and crocheting.

The mother said with tears like stones in her eyes: "Abed has gone and left behind three good sons. He taught them farm practices. Sharu will cultivate the land you granted to his father and his brothers will help him. I came to you seeking your kindness to accept them as agricultural workers in the farm. Look on them as your own beloved sons, and they will stand by you even unto death."

Misra: "Yes of course, I will be honored to have Abed's sons in my farm. I have no sons, I will be their second father."

Misra glanced at the young men examining them. With a sad frown on their faces, and tears in their eyes, Sharu looked hard and uncompromising. Salman looked huge with a sad smile on his face. Fawad was looking sadly at his feet with tears overflowing.

"I have an idea," said Misra addressing the mother. "Why don't you all move to the farm and live here for good?"

Mother: "That would be good for the land and the boys. I agree."
"I have a convenient place for you all. I have a spacious bungalow suitable for your accommodation."

Mother: "That would be good for the land and the boys. I agree."
"I have a convenient place for you all. I have a spacious bungalow suitable for your accommodation."

Mother: "That would be most generous of you."

Misra: "I heard that the brigand and his troops suffered a heavy loss; fifteen dead, and many others wounded. My farmers are not fighters. Who inflicted such tremendous loss?"

Mother: "My sons had been training in martial arts since their tender age."

Misra: "So they are the ones who fought the brigand and his bandits and inflicted all these losses?"

Mother: "Ask them."

Sharu: "We had to fight to defend ourselves."

Salman: "Time will come when we take revenge for the murder of our father."

Fawad: "We vowed to tear him into pieces when we got the chance."

Sharu took out a purse from his pocket and gave it to Misra. "This is the money from selling the crops and cattle. My father told me to give it to you before he breathed his last."

Misra: "Life comes down to honesty and doing what is right. Your father was loyal and honest. Follow in your father's footsteps. All I ask from you is loyalty, honesty and respect."

The girls lifted up their heads from their embroidery and looked at the boys. Mahudri saw Sharu handsome, stern and trustworthy. Ashwaria saw Salman manly, handsome, huge and quite robust. Sonam saw Fawad of the utmost beauty and surpassing loveliness.

The mother and her sons left the mud house in the village and moved to the spacious bungalow in Misra's farm.

CHAPTER 2

In the spacious courtyard of the farm house, Sharu and his brothers were practicing martial arts with sword and dagger. They were half naked leaving the upper part of their bodies uncovered. They all looked muscular, fit, and strong, in good shape and ripped. Their faces and chests glistened with sweat with the intensity of the sun

Sharu had lean muscles of a warrior. A piece of cotton cloth bound his long hair into a top knot. Salman was magnificent. The muscles in his chest were huge and very well formed. His shoulders and arms were massive yet smooth. His tight abs rippled down his flat belly. Fawad had a tall hard body with well-defined muscles. His satin skin was a deep golden tan. His black long hair falling to his shoulder behind.

The brothers wrestled with each other, and practiced sword and dagger fighting. They fought wielding two weapons at once, one in each hand.

Fawad demonstrated his archery skills when he sent his arrows into targets that were barely discernible to the naked eye. He hit a distant apple on his first try, and then split that arrow with his second shot.

Misra and his daughters Mahudri, Ashwaria, and Sonam watched the fighting and wrestling from the balcony. The girls were excited to watch the skills of the muscular and well-built young men in fighting and wrestling. Each girl looked at the man she chose fascinated.

Suddenly a 500 pounds bull escaped from its yard and caused terror whenever it went. The raging bull charged a farmer and trampled and gored him to death. The bull left the fatally injured man alone and attacked another farmer. The bull raised his head and tossed the farmer into the air. The farmer fell heavily to the ground to be trampled and gored repeatedly by the bull. The bull ripped open the belly of the second farmer leaving some of his insides bulging out.

Salman was immensely provoked. He shouted at the bull: "Hey! You monster, come and fight me if you can." The furious bull lowered his broad head to point his sharp horns at Salman. He scratched at the dirt and then charged, but to a man like Salman, the horns of a bull were just two convenient handles. Salman seized the bull by the horns and flipped him to the ground. Sharu came quickly and plunged his sword into the animal's heart. The Bull collapsed and died. Salman drew his dragger and cut off the Bull's right ear then climbed a tree close to the balcony, and presented the ear to Ashwaria as a token of affection. Ashwaria accepted the gift happily and smiled brightly at Salman. A frown rolled over Misra's face. He didn't like what Salman did.

Night falls and everyone gathers around the fire. The fire is the only source of light apart from the faint moonlight from the sky above. Misra and his daughters and brothers Khan gathered around the fire. The meat of the bull was roasted at the fire and eaten together with beans which were cooked by the mother. They all ate and laughed and listened to the beautiful voice of Fawad singing with his lyre:

> I love the way you look at me and smile
> Break the walls and enter my heart.
> Untie the chains and let love begins
> Draw me near and hold me tight
> I am glad to be yours

Sonam melted at his tender words finding it hard to believe not to be falling for him.

The Khan brothers became acquainted with the girls. Each boy fell in love with the girl of his choice.

Mahudri, a flower of beauty, was full of grace. The way she laughed as though she owned the moon; as though she owned the air around her. Mahudri was impressed by Sharu's strength and amazed by his wisdom. Sharu and Mahudri fell in love with each other. Mahudri became Sharu's joy. You find them pulling faces and chasing each other around the farm. Their laughter filled the air as they walked along the bank of the pond, splashing water on each other. They promenaded on donkey backs, and shared eating corn.   She melted in his arms, consumed by the raging fire of emotion his embrace never failed to ignite.

We hear Sharu singing a song of love and Madhudri dances to his song:

> You brought me happiness when before I was alone
> You brought me laughter when before I was in pain
> My heart lives inside of yours
> You are the one for me

Ashwaria was soft and tender as a rose petal. She was so delicate that if she sat beneath a tree and a leaf would fall and drift down and touch her skin, it would leave a bruise. Her eyes were as blue as the deep sea. She loved Salman and Salman adored her. If he looks in her eyes, his heart thunders in his chest. Salman towered over her as intense and savage as only he could be making her feel small and delicate in comparison. She loved him for being all tight muscle. She knew that he was a monster, but she wanted nothing more than a monster of her very own. With Salman she felt trapped in a cage, but she wanted to stay in his cage forever.

Salman and Ashwaria sat on the pond's bank looking at the water. Ashwaria began writing on the mud. Salman teased her by wiping out her mud writing. Ashwaria answered back by hitting his massive chest with her small hands. Salman blotted her face with mud, then carried her and threw her into the pond. He laughed crazily at seeing her struggling to get out of the water. She yelled at him hysterically. She was at the point of hating him now, but she loved being surrounded by his utter maleness. Salman kept laughing at her stupidly as if he had done nothing wrong.

Salman and Ashwaria played hide and seek for a kiss. The one that cannot be found after fifteen minutes of hiding will win the victory challenge and get a victory kiss from the looser. Salman always won and kissed Ashwaria all night. Ashwaria didn't care about winning because she loved Salman's warm kisses.

Salman sings for Ashwaria and she dances to his song:

> I want to be part of you
> I want to be all around you
> Draw me near and hold me
> Kiss my lips and touch my heart

Fawad loved Sonam and Sonam loved Fawad. Fawad was beautiful to look at. He was tall and handsome as hell. He had the most adorable eyes that bewitched Sonam and the cutest smile that took her breath away.

Fawad had the ability to make Sonam laugh every time he spoke. He filled up her soul with happiness and abundant love. With the most adorable smile on her face, she shouts in his face: "You're crazy. Maybe that's why we just make crazy together."

Fawad had a beautiful voice. He was clever in singing with his primitive lyre. A lyre made of a tortoise hollow shell and strings of sheep gut. He sang for Sonam melodies of his soul that were celebrated with cheerful dancing.

Fawad sings and Sonam dances:

When you look aside you put to shame the wild gazelle
And when you walk with a vacillating gait, the willow branch is envious
And when you display your countenance, you confound the sun and
the moon and captivates every beholder
Eve has not borne anyone like you

The girls felt loved, cherished and protected. They have found the men of their dream. Their love overflowed out of their pure souls like the streams of water that descend from a high mountain into a valley where the flowers are blooming and the plants are growing. With the strong love in their hearts, the three brothers worked hard in the farm, and the farm brought forth its pleasant crops and fruits.

CHAPTER 3

It was the habit of the girls to meet their lovers in the morning while working in the farm. If Sharu were cutting wood in the forest, and then loading the logs onto the wagon, Mahudri would drive the wagon to the farm and the famers would unload it and store the logs in the log store. It was her obsession to see Sharu chopping down a tree. His naked torso with every muscle moving with the blows of the axe fascinated her. When he sits to get some rest she hastens to wipe sweat from his brow. The scent of his manly sweat, thick in her nostrils, opening her sexual floodgates.

Sharu dances with Mahudri and sings:

> My beloved shames the full moon in beauty
> And surpasses in figure the slender branch
> Her absence is like the fire that burns my heart
> An in her presence I enjoy the garden of delight
> Her cheeks put roses to shame
> Her teeth have eclipsed pearls
> When you smile, honey wells from your lips.
> When you take a step the earth loses its balance.

I will love you for as long as the sun rises to flush the mountains
I was born when I met you
Truly you are unforgettable

Everything in Salman was big. His body was huge. His muscles were massive. His eyes were beautifully wide, and his jet black hair was thick and spreading back on his shoulder. He is strong like a bull and fights like a lion. His love was also overwhelming for it can contain the whole universe. His love to Ashwaria was so powerful that both of them were strongly enraptured with each other.

Salman cared for huge things like oxes and cows. He handled livestock. He goes out with the animals to the pastures early in the morning and in the end of the day he takes the animals back to their barn. Ashwaria milks the cows, with her tender fingers, and the cows surrender to her gentle milking.

The wide pasture became Salman and Ashwaria's playground. They shouted and yelled at each other jovially. They laughed so hard that they fall on the ground. Wrapped in each other's arms, they kissed and murmured words of love.

Salman had a smooth and dreamy voice. In merry tones he sings beautiful verses and Ashwaria dances to his song:

"God guard a face that is veiled with loveliness.
The full moon is its slave, and the stars are its servants.
Each one of your glances cause hearts to turn over.
Half of you is a ruby, a third is of jewels, a fifth of musk, and a
sixth of ambergris.
You were fashioned from mother-of-pearls, nay you are more splendid.

Fawad's role in the farm was to tend, feed and guard herds of sheep. He takes it to a green pasture that is good and fair. He moves from one place to another with the herds. You may find him in the valleys and the plains with Sonam laughing, jumping and mingling with the sheep. The best part was when Fawad plays with the lyre and sings melodious songs.

Fawad sings and Sonam dances to his melodious song:

Where it is said to me would you rather that you should behold her
Or a drought of pure water?
I would answer: "her."
Where it is said to me would you rather that you should behold her
Or to own the world?
I would answer: "her."

CHAPTER 4

Misra sat in the guest room thinking. The girls had grown up and are now ready for marriage. He had noticed that his daughters were strongly infatuated with brothers Khan. Brothers Khan are poor and were working in his farm as humble farmers. They do not derive from families of high social status. He had granted their father a small piece of land to live on, and when he died all his sons still live on the same land and the crops produced do not suffice their needs. It would be an utter disgrace if his precious daughters marry these poor primitive creatures. They knew nothing about civilized manners or etiquette. What would his distinguished relatives and friends say if the girls married these poor mumble farmers?

The girls must marry rich men of a similar social status. He must find suitable grooms for his three daughters. His daughters must marry in quick succession.

Misra called his daughters to discuss his future plans for them. The girls gathered with their father in the guest room.

Misra: "You have reached the age of marriage and it is about time that you get married. I will arrange family meetings to get you acquainted with family youth."

Mahudri: "Father, I have already chosen the man I want to live with for the rest of my life. I am not suitable to any but Sharu only."

Ashwaria: "I chose a man who can love me, cherish me and protect me against danger and evil."

Sonam: "I chose someone who won't give up on me no matter what. My heart beats only for him."

Misra: "And who are the men you have chosen as your future husbands?"

Madhuri: Sharu, Salman and Fawad."

Misra: "Oh! How nice? You have degraded to the level of choosing humble farmers as your husbands? This relationship isn't built to last."

Ashwaria: "They are honorable farmers and real men."

Misra: "Stop this nonsense. I am your father and I know where your happiness lies. You must marry men of a similar social status."

Mahudry: "Please respect our choices father."

Misra: "Enough Mahudri! Grow up and face the world. You do not understand. I am an old man. I fear I might die without you getting married."

Ashwaria: "Do not fear anything father. We love our men and they love us. They are capable of supporting and protecting us."

Sonam: "Happiness is to Love and be loved in return. Our men love us and they will make us happy."

"Shut up you fools." Misra sharply reprimanded his daughters.

"You must understand that the girls must marry, must belong to a man, without being asked when, who, or how. You have reached the age of marriage and it is time that you marry the men I will choose for you. No more arguments the matter is settled. Now get lost. I don›t want to see your faces around here for the rest of the week. You got it?"

The girls hurried up to the bungalow to warn their men about the intention of their father to marry them to strangers. The brothers were sitting at a low round table eating lunch. Sharu looked at Mahudri and realized that there was something serious she wanted to talk about. He smiled and pointed at the food saying: "Come girls and join us. Mother makes delicious food."

Each girl sat beside her man. Sharu fed Mahudri with his hand, and so did Fawad with Sonam. Salman however dished up Ashwaria's plate with plenty of food. Ashwaria laughed saying, "Take it easy Salman, a bit by bit, love."

Chaay was then served, then Sharu addressed the girls: "Now tell me what you have to say."

Mahudri talked on their behalf: "Father wants to marry us to strangers, men we do not love, rich men of our social status."

The bad news were extremely unpleasant and shocking to the brothers. A sad frown were drawn on their faces expressing sadness and worry.

Sharu said sorrowfully: "If we are poor God will enrich us from His grace."

Salman said furiously: "I will smash the head of anyone comes near my girl."

"I will pierce the eye of anyone comes near Sonam." Fawad said angrily.

Sharu: "Richness is not in the quantity of possessions that one has; true wealth is the richness of one's self. The best sustenance that we are given is that which is sufficient".

Salman: "We live not of the labor of other men's hands, nor of the sweat of other men's brows. We eat our bread by the labor of our own hands."

Fawad: "A lot of things money can never buy. Blessings and prosperity will be ours because we eat our bread justly and lawfully."

Sharu: "The contentment of the heart is what makes a person realize and appreciate true richness. Whoever amongst you wakes up, secure in his home, healthy in his body, having the bare amount of food that he requires for the day, then it is as if the entire world has been captured for him, with all that it contains!"

Sharu glanced at Madhuri and continued: "We are content with what we have. We rejoice in the way things are. In fact there is nothing lacking, the world belongs to us."

Mahudri: "I want to live this life of contentment with you Sharu. I don't mind living with you in suffering and ease as long as we are together."

Ashwaria: "Living with the man I love under all circumstances is what I long for."

Sonam: "I want to share life's beauty with Fawad. It is sufficient for me to have a corner in his heart, and a nap undisturbed in his arms."

Sharu: "Let our hopes not our hurts shape our future. We must learn to sail in high winds. We must be prepared for the worst, but hope for the best. If we believe that tomorrow will be better, we can bear a hardship today. We must go forward with hope and not backward by fear."

"Sharu, the always wise." Fawad said laughing.

Sharu: "Ladies, do not fear anything. You will be our wives and the mother of our children. You will put into the mouths of your children the bread that our own hands have earned."

The words of Sharu comforted the girls and appeased their terror.

"Now, let's enjoy ourselves. Let's choose happiness over hurt." Sharu shouted joyously.

Sonam: "Yes let's be happy forever and ever. Let's be cheerful."

Fawad:" Let's take a walk in the woods and walk by the river."

They left the bungalow and walked through the fields until they reached the woods. The sun was shining through the trees. They could feel the rays of the sun on their skin giving a warming sensation. The birds sat on the trees and sang sweetly. The plants and all the trees around, swayed with the wind as if were blessing the joy of the lovers.

"Fawad, I missed your beautiful voice. Recite to me some verses." Sonam said laughing merrily.

Fawad: "Fine, but only if you sing with me."
Sonam: "Sure."

Fawad

I saw her walking in coquetry
my heart said tik tik tik
Sonam

He knocked on my heart tak tak tak
My heart beats faster tik tik tik
Sonam
I wished he hadn't knocked on my door tak tak tak
For my heart still beats tik tik tik

Fawad

My heart ached with joy of her nearness
It ceased not to beat tik tik tik

Sonam
My heart skipped a beat from ecstasy
He filled my life with tik tik tik
Fawad

I wish I haven't knocked on her door
I can't stop my heart from beating tik tik tik

Ashwaria: "Salman, recite to me some verses perhaps my chest may
thereby be dilated."
Salman: "Okay, but you dance to my song."
Ashwaria: "Okay.
Salman sings and Ashwaria dances.

Salman
Slender of waist and supple of ankle
You walk in beauty and sways in coquetry
Your eyes like those of a deer
Firing arrows scorching my heart

Mahudri: "Sharu dear, sing to me. Perhaps the sad thoughts in my
heart be dispelled."

Sharu: "I sing, and you dance to my song O lover of my soul."
Madhuri: "I will dance to the rhythm of your heartbeat."
Sharu sang and Mahudri danced and sang.

Sharu
your sparkling earrings and shining anklets are beautiful to see
your dazzling smile makes me dance like I have never danced before
Looking in your eyes is as though staring inside diamonds

Mahudri
Stop being so sweet
I am frightened that if I touch you
I will fall apart
Sharu

I do not enjoy the sight of the world but by your sight
You are a precious pearl in shells contained
I am ready to lay my life at your feet

CHAPTER 5

Sharu went to the forest to shop wood. Mahudri accompanied him. It was a pleasure for her to see him chopping the trees. She sat on a log watching him work. He was so soaked in sweat that his shirt clung to his body outlining every muscle. She could smell his sweat mingled with the odor of wood. Sharu took his shirt off and tossed it over a tree branch to dry. Mahudri was impressed by the play of muscles in his arms and chest as he wielded the axe. She found herself yearning to feel his strong arms holding her close and his mouth, sweet and strong on hers. She walked over slowly to him and grabbed him from behind and held him dearly. He turned to face her. His face broke into a dazzling smile. His smile delighted and warmed her heart.

"I am drowned in sweat!" He said apologizing.

"You breathe gentle sweet-smelling. You smell good, you smell wood. I want to breathe in your scent. I want to share your bed. I want you to explore the curves of my body. I want to be only yours, I want you to be my man." She said savoring his masculine scent.

"I couldn't imagine life without you." She said kissing his lips. Her kiss was ardent and he returned it with equal passion.

"I want to be the reason you smile. I want to be the man you rely on. I want you to be the mother of my children." He said cupping her cheeks with both hands and looking intently in her eyes.

"I want to propose to your father. Do you think he will accept me as a son in law?" a sudden worry ceased his face.

"Try to persuade him. He might accept your proposal. Father is a good man after all. He will not find another man better than you. You are wise, noble and brave."

"I am poor. I cannot give you what a rich man can."

"All the riches cannot buy happiness."

"But neither can poverty." He said testing her.

"Love is sufficient for us. Love will direct our course. We would seek only love's peace and love's pleasure."

Her words touched him deeply. He said feeling a lump in his throat: "Yes darling but love's ways are hard and steep. I can only feed you the fruit of the labor of my hands. Can you accept this kind of hard life?"

She kissed his lips passionately then looked in his eyes and said with tears running down her cheeks: "We will be like a running brook that sings its melody to the night. We will wake up at dawn to give thanks for another day of loving. We will fear the Lord and walk in his way."

He gathered her in his arms and held her tightly to his chest. "I love you with all my heart and soul. I love you more than my own life." He said with tears in his eyes: "I am happy Mahudri. Very happy. Let's sing and dance.

They both sang and danced:

Sharu
Go out and tell the world
You have filled my heart with sunshine
and your love has given me joy
Go out and tell the world
I have been blessed with an angel from above
Out of Eden God has sent you to me

Mahudri
Come into my heart and stay
You are all I need to know.
You are my shelter you are my rock
Without you I have no place to go

Sharu
In your presence there is peace and joy
In your love I live and die
You gave me a new birth

Sharu and his brothers decided to ask master Misra for the hand of his daughters in marriage, but they were afraid of being rejected, and return broken-hearted. The brothers gathered in the guest room fearing Misra's anger and rage.

"Sharu and his brothers are in the guest room asking to see you." One of Misra's servants announced. Misra frowned fiercely and with signs of fury on his face stormed into the guest room.

Misra: "What brought you in this hour? What do you want from me?"
Sharu: "Sir we came to ask your daughters hand in marriage."

Misra was caught off-guard. "Oh! How considerate of you." He said scornfully.

Sharu glanced at his feet and said timidly: "It is not permissible for a woman to get married without the permission of her guardian Sir."

"Usually girls have little knowledge and experience of life and what is best for them, and they may be deceived by some nice words, and be ruled by their hearts rather than by their heads. You loved my daughters behind my back. You have exploited them. You deceived them with your honey talks and sweet songs." Misra said enraged.

Sharu: "We are not of the people of treachery. We honored your daughters. They are pure, intact and virgin. Marriage should be honored by all, and the marriage bed must be kept pure."

"And how do you plan to support them?" Misra said mockingly.

Sharu: "We sow the seeds, we cultivate the land and water the plants. We grow our food and eat it with the sweat of our brows. Our food suffices for all because we mention God's name over it before we eat."

Fawad: ""We do not think there is anything better for two who love one another than marriage. Love is more important than money."

Salman: Love doesn't hurt. Marriage is not wealth but kind and understanding. I love Ashwaria. I will protect her and stand up for her."

Sharu: "We believe in marriage, commitment, togetherness, love and family."

Misra: "That is not enough. I know what is best for my daughters and who is best suited to marry them. My daughters will marry rich husbands from wealthy families. And they will do what I say. The girls should not go against their father's opinion."

The moments Sharu shared with Madhuri clouded his mind along with tears in his eyes. "I loved Mahudri from the moment I saw her. She is the love of my life. Please do not deprive me of her." Sharu said with voice cracking with emotions.

Fawad: "I love Sonam and Sonam loves me. I am begging you sir, please let your daughters marry the men they have chosen."

Salman begging: "I love Ashwaria. She is everything I ever wanted. She is my life. She brings joy to my heart. I will cherish her always and forever."

Misra: "I will marry my girls to people of high social class. You are just poor farmers. You cannot afford my daughters high expenses."

Sharu: We work hard, for by labor are the sweets of life obtained."

Salman: "Money cannot buy love, nor save a marriage. Ashwaria is the comfort I need, the embrace that cures; she is my passion, my smile, and my laugh."

Fawad: "You blame us for falling for your daughters! Love is an illumination. Love is inspiring. A flower cannot blossom without sunshine, and man cannot live without love. Do not deprive your daughters from what they love. Let them marry whom they please."

Misra: You are not equals. You are unfit and no match for my daughters. I will marry my daughters to those who are like them in dominion, rank and descent. You hurt me when you asked for my daughters' hand in marriage. My answer is no, absolutely not."

Sharu: "It is unlawful for the father to force his daughter to marry someone she does not want. The virgin should not be given in marriage until her permission has been sought."

Fawad: "There is no religion which support the practice of forced marriage. You should only give your daughters in marriage for their own interests, not for your own."

Salman: You have to fear God with regard to your daughters and not give them in marriage to anyone except those with whom they are pleased from among men who are compatible and suitable."

Misra: "You are not compatible or suitable. My daughters have wealth, riches and honor, far above your wildest dreams. Wealth provides opportunity to find greater fulfillment in life and you are poor."

Sharu: "Contentment is far more valuable than riches. Once our basic needs have been met, money contributes very little to our overall happiness and well-being. Gratitude, generosity, and contribution produce far more. And that is the real goal: to live lives of joy and fulfillment and help others to do the same.

Fawad: "Your daughters are virtuous. Their price is far above rubies."

Sharu took a breath for patience. He said after a moment's hesitation: "You will destroy your daughters by your stubbornness. You will watch them go to pieces and your heart will break for them, but you won't be able to help them."

"Your words are as good as dirt. Get out of here, get out of my sight, you make me sick to look at you." Misra said angrily glancing at the three brothers in contempt.

The three brothers endured all the cruel words and criticism Misra threw at them and left downhearted broken.

Misra imprisoned the three girls in their rooms and appointed chamberlains to guard them and forbid them leaving the house.

The three brothers sat on the bank of the river talking about their misfortune.

Sharu: "The hardest thing to do is watch the one you love marry someone else. I am an emaciated waif who is neither dead nor alive.

Salman: "I still fall for her every day. She is the pulse that throbs in my veins. She is the rhythm of my heart beat."

Fawad: "Not a night goes by and she is not in my dreams. I would be a fool not to notice the way the sunshine played with her hair."

Sharu: "My heart is broken in hundred pieces. I gave my soul to her but it all ended in so much pain."

Salman: "I long for her touch and her warm embrace, the look of her eyes, the smile on her face."

Sharu: "She meant the world to me. She will always be in my heart forever. My love for her will remain unchanged, undiminished, nor will I ever stop thinking of her."

Salman: "I must see her and press her to my heart. I love her to the point of madness, I cannot continue to be separated from her."

Fawad: "Forget her name, forget her face, forget her warm embrace. Now she will marry someone new."

Sharu: "No Fawad, don't say that. Love is a gentle embrace between body and soul. Love is a caress of two souls. Love is a great passion between hungry hearts. Love gave us all that."

Salman: "I had no idea that the heart could cause such trouble and strife. She meant the world to me. I love her still."

Sharu: "I don't have much to say just silent tears."

Salman: "She gave me so much strength and yet she is my only weakness."

Fawad: "What resources has the archer when in meeting the enemy, he desires to discharge the arrow, but finds his bow-string broken?

Salman: "Calamities of separation descended on us all, consuming us so heavily. Tell me Sharu, what's the remedy?

Sharu: "Everything happens by faith and destiny. Let's endure with patience the life our fates decree."

CHAPTER 6

Abhay Agrahari is an owner of a large farm fifteen miles away from Misra's farm. Abhay and Misra were good friends. They both came from a landlord, aristocratic milieu. Abhay had an only son called Shyam Agrahari. Abhay was sick at heart as he thought of the evil nature of Shyam's vices. Shyam was debauched in his life, extravagant with the allowance he takes from his father, a gambler, a confirmed drunkard, one fond of low men and of low women. Shyam was born of wine and drunkenness. Alcohol brought him to filthy fornication.

There was not a pub or a public house in all the area he had not visited. He got into bad companies with evil people he knew in the pubs. They got him drunk to take advantage of him and force him to pay their booze. If he resisted they beat him pretty near to death and steal his money. His companions did not see him as a human being to be respected but an object to be exploited. He spent his money on them, and in spite of that, they always stole his money while he was drunk!

Shyam was also a sadist getting pleasure from inflicting pain. He not only lacked empathy but enjoyed inflicting harm on others. He was always bad tempered and nasty to other people as a child. When he grew older, he experienced pleasure from watching others undergo discomfort or pain, and took enjoyment in performing sadistic acts.

Shyam was totally unpredictable. He felt good about himself when he was in charge. He looked at women as an instrument of sexual pleasure; a commodity without regard to their personality or dignity.

Shyam was a gambler too. He used to bet thousands of rupees on dices. When his father deprived him from his allowance, he hit him with a stick until it was broken. People hated Shyam because of his sins and vices.

Shyam's alcoholism became so bad that his father had to go search for him in the alleys, cheap pubs, and door ways. After a lengthy search, he finally found him asleep on the steps of one of the pubs. Shyam had reached rock bottom.

Due to high operation costs and poor crop prices, as well as Shyam's neglect of the farm, in addition to wasting the farm income on gambling and drinking, a huge debt had been entailed on the farm, and Abhay was about to lose his livelihood.

Abhay borrowed more as farm income went down, and now he had several creditors hot on his heels. He cannot repay the debts he owed to creditors.

Abhay analyzed the situation and realized that the farm was going down into bankruptcy. The best way to save the farm and be out of debt is to marry his stubborn rebellious son to a rich woman. This will pay off his debts, and save the property from dangerous hands. Thoughts crowded quick into his mind. Marriage would certainly reform Shyam. Shyam would surely be a better person if he becomes a husband responsible for a wife and children. A good wife from a decent family might keep Shyam on track.

Abhay called occasionally to see his friend Misra, the landlord of the nearby prosperous farm. Misra had three beautiful daughters, the eldest seemed wise and was about his son's age. She could be a suitable wife for Shyam, his reckless wild son.

Abhay called his son Shyam and reprimanded him saying: "You are always drunk. You spend your money on fools in pubs. The farm became unproductive because of your extravagance and neglect. Now the farm is under heavy debt loads. I am going to sell it to pay the debt. It's about time that you focus on the things that matter.

Shyam: "What are the things that matter?"

Abhay: "To marry a rich woman who will love you and builds you up."

Shyam: "I'm going to marry for love."

Abhay: "Marriages were made for strategic alliances, economic gain, familial ties, and a variety of other unromantic reasons."

Shyam: "Do you have any particular girl in mind?"

Abhay: "Yes. Prepare yourself for a long trip tomorrow. You will meet someone with the financial means to support you and straightens you up."

Abhay paid his old friend Misra a visit. Misra welcomed him heartedly. Abhay introduced his son saying: "Shyam, show your uncle due respect."

Shyam touched Misra's feet in due respect.
Tea was served with cake slices and Misra and his guests began to talk.

Abhay: "I want to ask for your blessing before my son Shyam officially propose to you. I want my son to marry your daughter. Shyam asks you for the hand of your daughter in marriage."

Misra shut his eyes and sighed in utter happiness. He said exhilarating: "Why of course you have my blessing. I am enchanted to meet you and your boy."

Abhay: "So you agree?"

Misra: "The Agrahari family is a prominent wealthy family. I can't imagine a better man than Shyam to marry my daughter. Welcome to the family Shyam."

Misra got out of his chair and went to the hallway and called aloud: "Mahudri. You come down quickly. I want you to meet my guests."

Mahudri came after a few moments to see her father conversing merrily with his guests.

Misra: "Mahudri my daughter; this is my dear friend Abhay and his son Shyam. Shyam is here to ask for your hand in marriage."

She felt betrayed. She wanted to scream but she remained silent so not to embarrass her father. She sat trembling allover. She stared at Shyam. Hate spewed out of her. This is not the man she wanted to spend her life with. No man could ever replace Sharu in her heart. She stared at him. She didn't like the nasty looks he shot at her from red sneaky eyes.

She felt ill. She excused herself and ran into her room, curled into a ball, and dissolved into tears.

After Abhay and his son left, Misra visited his daughter in her room. She confronted him: ""How could you do this to me? I am your daughter!" She shouted.

Misra: "My obligation as a father is to see you happily married. You should be thankful to God because He has brought you a man from a decent family. Cheer up. Every girl dreams of getting married. Parents dream of seeing their girl getting married."

Mahudri weeping: "I love Sharu. I don't want to marry someone else."

Misra: "Shut up you naughty girl. Do not utter his name before me again. Having this lowly man as a son in law is a disgrace to our family. Do not demean yourself by marrying someone of lowly origin."

Mahudri: "Wrong father. Sharu is compassionate, and a gentleman. He is wise and prudent. He fights to protect us against evil. He cultivates our land. He is concerned about our wellbeing. We are practically nothing without Sharu and his brothers."

Misra: "Sober up my child. Be realistic. You are too good for him. His station in life is far below yours. Get your mind off him. Shyam is the right man for you I am sure. I chose for you the best of men."

Mahudri: "I don't love him father. Don't coerce me into a marriage against my will."

Misra: "First come marriage, then comes love. You will learn to love him."

Mahudri: "You have killed my dreams. You've killed everything inside me. Don't you have any compassion? I am better off dead. I'd rather die. There is nothing left. Go ahead and marry me off. I will kill myself." She sobbed in grief.

Angry at her obstinacy, he slapped her face and screamed in her face: "There is no going back. The marriage had been set up."
Misra left the room in anger and slapped the door shut after him.
Misra locked Mahudri in her room, refusing to let her out until her wedding day.

The wedding was quickly organized and took place in the big hall, which was preoccupied with Nobel men; and in it were all kinds of flowers and all kinds of sweet scents, and varieties of fresh fruits, together with abundance of various kinds of exquisite viands, and beverages prepared from the choicest grape-vines.

Sharu and his brothers did not attend the wedding. Sharu's anxiety and grief increased on account of Madhuri's marriage to another man. Salman and Fawad became extremely frustrated. The obstinacy of Misra made them realize that it was not certain that they will marry the girls they loved.

Mahudri was brought from her room. She felt as if she were driven to the guillotine. At the end of the wedding ceremony, Asha and two maids accompanied Mahudri to her room. Shyam was already there smiling. He anticipated a hot steamy night with a virgin and not with experienced prostitutes as he usually do. But he must get drunk first. That was his habit before having sex with cheap women.

Shyam put a large smile on his face and said to Mahudri: "I will be with you in an hour. Take your time I am not in a hurry."

He then went to the nearest pub and drank wine profusely. He was so drunk that he staggered all the way home. Mahudri saw before her a drunken man. His eyes were glassy and bloodshot. He had troubles keeping his eyes open. He couldn't walk a straight line.

In their first night together, like an uncontrollable beast he grabbed her and ripped off her underwear. When she resisted him he used force to hold her in position. She tried to push him off her, but this excited him more, he grabbed both her arms, and flung them above her head, held them there and quickly forced open her legs and raped her.

"I hate you. Damn you! I am in agony, I am so brutally misused. Let me go", she cried out while desperately trying to wiggle away.

As Mahudri kept resisting him each time he touched her, Shyam became extremely violent as he continued raping her over the next days.

Mahudri begged: "Please stop you are hurting me." But he continued to rape her until she vomited. Her vomit infuriated him, so he punched her and sunk his teeth into her neck inflicting deep wounds.

When he finished, she lay sobbing in the bed. He shouted at her: "shut up." But she couldn't. So he yelled at her: Shut up whore, be quiet slut."

During the next months, Mahudri was subjected to vicious assaults physically and sexually. Every night Shyam came like a bull hungry for sex. He always came drunk and took her by force. He stuffed her underwear down her throat before raping and punching her repeatedly. Mahudri passed out several times. She believed she was going to die.

Shyam spent several days drinking in pubs and enjoying cheap women. Mahudri was glad to have some time away from him. She laid on a chase long sofa and closed her eyes trying not to remember the nightmares she had with him. The thought of him coming again to assault her scared her. He made her feel with the passing days that she was completely worthless – like an object, instead of a human being.

She opened her eyes to see Shyam standing before her. He leaned to kiss her. She pulled herself up and staggered to her feet.

"Get out of my sight right now. You are drunk." She demanded loudly.

"You abomination, you vilest, most hateful woman, damn you. How dare you treat me like that? I am your master, I am your God." Signs of anger spread across his face.

He closed his hand into a tight fist and punched her face knocking her out onto the floor. He snatched her up by the hair and carried her to bed. Tears began to fall as she realized that she was fighting a losing battle. He threw her on the bed and shouted: "Surrender you slut; all women are sluts."

"You love being chocked and slapped across your face eh? I know your type. To get horny you like being tortured. You like me to treat you like a dirty slut eh?

She twisted her body in every direction she could manage. He slapped her face hard. It hurt, but she kept struggling. He slapped again much harder. She stopped fighting; her body went limp. Tears rolled out of her puffed up eyes. She surrendered letting out weak moans of pain.

He savagely tore off her clothes exposing her naked body. He centered his body between her thighs then worked his way up with spanking, biting, hair pulling, dirty talk and slapping every part of her body he could reach.

Mahudri was in extreme pain. The force of his rape was damaging her body. He was raping her so hard, that she started hemorrhaging inside. Her pain seemed to only fuel his lust. When he finished with her, he climbed from on top of her, and stood over her taking pride in her pain.

Mahudri's only consolation and relief was to cry on Asha's shoulder and complain to her about her mischief.

Mahudri: "Asha, you are the only one around that I can complain to."

Asha: "Complain all you like. I know it was bad, and you held up well. You should be proud of yourself."

Mahudri: "He derives sexual enjoyment from torturing me. He gets his sexual enjoyment from being violent and causing pain. He forces me to bed by punching, slapping and kicking. During sex he beats me, bites my flesh and pulls my hair. My body is abused and tortured for his pleasure. He doesn't care about my feelings. He treats me like crap, like shit. I can't bear his body's weight upon my breast. " Mahudri said crying.

Asha: "How could you accept this? Why don't you tell your father?"

"He threatens me all the time that he was going to hurt me more if I refuse any of his sexual commands or called out for help."

After each horrible sexual assault, Mahudri sends for Asha to attend to her wounds. Asha sits by Mahudri's side and gives her a strong, enough dose of liquid Datura to make her sleep. The experienced Asha then cleans the wounds by using a mixture of various ingredients containing honey as an antibacterial agents, lint as an absorbent and grease as a barrier against contamination.

Mahudri lived in silence with this repeated emotional and physical abuse. Her final source of consolation was the anticipation of her own death.

CHAPTER 7

Asha met Misra in the living room. She commenced a conversation with him.

Asha: "Master Misra, Mahudri has a lot to talk to you about. It's important that you listen to her."

Misra: "She wants to talk to me! What about?"

Asha: "About her life with her husband."

Misra: "I could hear their loud voices as if they were quarrelling. But this is their own life, no one must interfere."

Asha: "I raised her, I care about her. I want you to open your heart to her and ease her suffering."

Misra annoyed: "Suffering! Is she suffering?"

Asha: "Yes she is. Just listen to her."

Misra worried: "Tell her I am ready to talk to her at any time she wishes."

Mahudri came hesitant to talk to her father. She was embarrassed to talk to him about such a delicate matter. She sat before him, head down looking at the ground between her feet. She did not say anything; she glanced at him then looked down again. She began to cry.

Misra: "What's up Mahudri? What do you want to talk to me about?"

She peered up at him.

Misra: "You definitely are a sight for sore eyes." He said worried

Mahudri: "I regret I am under the necessity to inform you that I have been wronged."

Misra: "What do you mean?"

Mahudri: "My husband is the vilest man alive. He is evil, rotten, mean and nasty."

Misra: "What happened between you and him, explain to me."

Mahudri: "You afflicted me with this man and that I have experienced from him was done on your account."

Misra: What has he done? Tell me everything."

Mahudri: "He made me feel dirty and like trash at the end of each sexual encounter. I feel like I had been raped many times. He slaps me, punches me, and threatens me during sex. I have had enough of this shit."

Misra: "Why does he treat you so badly? You must have rebelled against him."

Madhuri: "I hate everything about him. That is not a marriage, it is oppression and abuse. Marriage requires acceptance. Without it the marriage is a sham, a disgrace, a dishonor like living in adultery."

Misra: "I see him a decent man. He treats me politely, and talks to me gently.

Madhuri: "He can conceal his injustice with rhetoric. Anyone who is dishonest but speaks well deserves the greatest censure. "

Misra: "A woman must not challenge her husband."

Mahudri: "How do you support him so blindly?

Misra: He is a good man. Don't annoy him. Stay out of his way. Your destiny had been pre-determined. You cannot escape your doom."

Mahudri: "You abused me and forced me to marry an evil man. You never considered that consent of the woman is necessary. You forced me to marry a man I hate."

Misra: "I chose the most suitable man for you."

Mahudri: "You deceived me in the cruelest possible manner father. You deserted me and cast me into the hands of a man you knew will defile me – a man you knew will twist and pervert everything good in me. The man you married me to is the world's most wicked man."

She realized that the hope that her father would stand by her was gone. He chose to trust Shyam and take his side. Women in his opinion are nothing but slaves to their husbands; to be persecuted and ravished without resisting or opposing.

Mahudri left her father heading to her room. The ugly words of Shyam resonated in her ears: "I am your master, I am your God."

Shyam came to Mahudri every night stumbling drunk, throwing up drunk and passed out on the bed.

CHAPTER 8

It was the first time that Sharu knew that Shyam was an avid wine drinker when he left the house for days without telling where he was going.

Misra and Mahudri were dining in the dining room when Misra asked his servant to bring him Sharu. It was the first time that Sharu entered the house after the wedding. Sharu stood before the dining table looking at Misra and his daughter. Mahudri was extremely embarrassed and couldn't face Sharu's sad eyes. She cast her eyes in her plate unable to look at him directly.

Misra: "Shyam left the house for days and I want you to help me get him back."

Sharu: "I don't know where to find him. I don't know his whereabouts."

Mahudri lifted her eyes from her plate and looked at Sharu with eyes clouded with pain. Sharu read the truth in her eyes – she was sad, she was not happy.

"Search for him in the pubs and public houses." She said feeling extremely embarrassed. She then looked down staring into her plate pretending to eat.

"O shut up Mahudri. You have reduced your husband to the status of the lowest of the low." Misra shot at her.

Sharu left to search for Shyam. He searched for him in all the pubs and public houses in the area until he found him in a pub sleeping on a table. He carried him on his shoulder and put him up before him on his horse and drove back to the farm. Sharu carried him to the bedroom and put him to bed. Carrying Shyam back home drunk seemed like an endless process.

One night after midnight, Sharu brought him home like a dead man. Sharu placed him on the bed. Mahudri was met with the stench of drunken vomit. She stood far from Shyam staring at him disgustingly.

After what seemed an eternity, Shyan stumbled to his feet with much effort and moaning. He sat on bed trying to steady the spinning. He threw up again.

"Sorry Mahudri. I didn't know you were suffering that much." Sharu said regretfully.

"I didn't want him back. Why did you bring this garbage here?" She yelled hysterically at Sharu.

Sharu: "Mahudri please calm down."

Mahudri weeping: "I don't want to see him. I want to forget this entire period of my life. He wrecked my life. I have lost all pleasure in living. I want to die."

Sharu: "I am sorry Mahudri. I am awfully sorry. I couldn't ever imagined he was so bad. I'm not trying to get in the way or anything, but please don't lose faith."

She yelled at him: "O please spare me your nonsense. Can't you see how devastated I am? I feel sorry for myself. What I have done wrong being punished like this? I am forever torn. Life without you is a terrible fright. I live in dirt. The only hope left is that you take all this dirt away. Can you clean this dirt? Of course you can't. We have been drifted apart. We are not together anymore."

She continued crying: "What am I doing here? Everything is cold and dark. I can't live this life. I don't belong here. Do you actually want to see me like this – surrounded by dirt? Leave me alone to face my suffering and pain. Go and don't ever come back."

With all the sadness in the world Sharu gave her a bow, then turned on his heel and left.

Misra heard Mahudri's weeping, he came in haste to see what was going on. He knew at a glance that Shyan was awfully drunk.

Misra: "Shyan sober up we need to talk." He said tapping heavily on Shyam's shoulders. Shyan stared at him with deflected eyes.

Misra: "What in the world is wrong with you? You are not going to come into my house drunk every night. You need to find some place to live."

Shyam could barely string four or five words together. He said with difficulty: "I feel sorry for myself because I am facing financial difficulties."

Misra: "I will not let you use whatever you are going through to make excuses for your cruelty and addiction. Deal with your problems rather than make problems for me and your wife. You are despicable and ugly."

Shyam: "Despise me as much as you please; I am a worthless, cowardly wretch."

Misra: "You occupied yourself with delights and pleasures and drinks. But you could not control your craziness, never ceases to abuse your wife."

Shyam: "Be not angry with me for my former offences; for forgiveness is required of the generous."

Misra: "I used to think you a man of good sense who attempted not aught but what was right, and uttered not aught but what was just. But you disappointed me. Where is your reason? You are of little sense and judgment."

Shyam: "Please be kind enough as to forgive me."

Misra: "Do not beguile me with your soft words. Stop drinking wine for it is the source of all evil."

Shyam: Please forgive me. Release me from a painful burden."

Misra: "I knew the financial crisis your father was going through. He is in terrible debt. Instead of helping your father run the farm, you have wasted your life on women and wine. Your debauchery and recklessness, and long neglecting of the farm are what made your father put the farm on the market. He now hopes for a speedy sale to satisfy the huge debt."

Misra continued reproaching him: "You don't have a house to shelter your wife, you don't have work of your own, you are completely broke. You married my daughter for her money. I didn't mind because you came from an decent family. I supported you, I gave you a handsome monthly allowance to look decent and honorable before the people, but you wasted it on wine and cheap women. You spread debauchery everywhere. You became contemptible."

Misra yelled at him: "What is lacking you to be a nice man? In my house you are in the utmost affluence, yet I find nothing from you but perfidy. From now on you will not get any allowances from me. Do something useful. Be a man and work for a living."

CHAPTER 9

It was one of the worst moments of Ashwaria and Sonam's lives: the morning their father suddenly announced that in about a week's time they would have to get married.

Ashwaria and Sonam argued with their father.

Ashwaria: "I don't want to marry against my will."

Sonam Shouted: "No" and fought back tears.

Misra: "No, you have to. You don't have a choice. Everyone gets married like this. You're not special. "

Ashwaria: "Father, how could a betrayal like this happen?"

Sonam: "Don't force me to marry someone against my will." Her heart skipped a beat.

Misra: "Your age is the perfect age to get married. People are starting to talk. Failing to arrange a marriage for you would surely cause me to lose status. I have a special responsibility to safeguard the family's reputation. Wedding celebrations are so expensive that when you marry one daughter, you generally marry the rest in the same go. The father of the men I chose for you is a respected elder in the village."

Ashwaria: "I have the right to choose my husband. This is center to my dignity and equality as a human being."

Sonam: "I must have the freedom to make a choice. Father you are putting so much pressure on me. "

Misra: "I have set the marriage up. Your fiancés will arrive tomorrow to make your acquaintance." Misra then left leaving the two girls crying out in grief.

Sonam said still sobbing: "The only way to survive this coercion is to flee. I will find a way to leave."

Ashwaria said through her tears: "I will tell Salman about this misfortune and see what he was going to say."

Sonam left the house and escaped to the woods. She stayed in the woods for days not willing to go back home. She loved Fawad and didn't want to face the same destiny Mahudri has had with Shyam. Misra got mad. The fiancés are coming tomorrow and the girls are being resentful, and on top of that, Sonam had left the house and escaped to the woods!

Misra knew that Sonam only responds to Fawad, so he called him and asked him to search for her and bring her home.

Fawad inquired: "Why did she escape?"

Misra: "I arranged two marriages for Ashwaria and Sonam. The fiancés are coming tomorrow to see the brides. Sonam left the house for two days now. Probably she escaped to the woods."

Fawad: "Again! You want to marry your daughters to strangers they knew nothing about?"

Misra said angrily: "It is strictly family business; do not interfere. Just do what you are told."

Fawad walked to the woods searching for Sonam. As he went on his way, Salman met him.

Salman: "Where to? Why leaving in such a hurry? You look worried!"

Fawad: "Misra arranged two marriages for Ashwaria and Sonam. The men he chose are coming tomorrow. Sonam escaped to the woods. I am going to find her."

Salman frowned. "This man is ruining his daughters by forcing them to marry against their will. Sonam decided she had enough. And that was it she was gone. Enough what happened to Madhuri. Her father plagued her with that monster spreading mischief in the land. I will not allow this to happen to Ashwaria and Sonam. Make haste and bring Sonam safe home. I will take care of the two men. Meet me tomorrow here, we are going to have some words with Misra."

Fawad traced Sonam's footsteps. Her footsteps ended at a tree. She had climbed up a tree and hid among the leafy branches.

He heard her melodious voice coming from above the tree: "Good morning my beautiful prince."

He laughed. She looked like a naive child playing seek and hide. "Come down to my arms beautiful princess." He opened his arms for her.

She came down and threw herself joyously into his arms. She kissed his lips and held him tight to her bosom. "I knew that you will come for me. What kept you so long? I felt like a fugitive up there."
"I came the moment your father asked me to get you back."

"I am not going back. I will live with you in the woods, in the mountains, up in the sky, down into the ocean, but I am not going back."

He kissed her hair, her eyes, and her neck. She looked at his wide black eyes, strong jaw and wide cheekbones and sighed deeply. His body brought welcomed heat to her own.

"It's been lonely days away from you. Tell me something beautiful." She muttered.

"Sonam." He said.

"O God. You don't know how much I love you. My life revolves around you. Don't leave me to strangers. Don't let me down, you are all I have got."

"I will not let your father dictates your choices. I will always be there for you. You can always count on me."

Fawad wanted to distract her from the bad thoughts. "Have you ever seen deer hunting?" He said.

"My love, have a nice hunting I will wait for you here."

"No. You will come with me."

"I am not used to such kind of adventure."

"It will be fun I assure you." He insisted.

They crested a steep hill and stopped for water. They drank from a small spring then continued their walk. They spotted a deer about fifty yards away. Fawad trotted slowly towards it and shot it with his bow. The arrow went through and penetrated deep into the center of the neck. The deer ran hard for 30 yards, then slowed to a staggering walk. His tail twitched erratically as it did its best to stay on its feet. Moments later, he fell and lay motionless.

Fawad slit the deer's throat before it is dead. He then removed the entrails and the inner loins. The deer was then hung upside down from a tree and Fawad began the skinning process. Fawad started from the top and worked his way down to the head. Once he finished, he cut some meat.

Fawad picked the best steaks for grilling – the back strap. He cut it into individual steaks. He then prepared a hardwood fire for grilling. The hardwood fire gave the most wonderful steaks because it grilled and smoked at the same time.

Fawad cut the grilled meat into small pieces, and fed Sonam with his own hand. She enjoyed being fed with his own hand.

"Excellent meal. I appreciate the effort you underwent to make it special for me. That means a lot to me. You made me feel beautiful and wanted." She said smiling sadly.

He hugged her close and kissed her lips. "I love you." She whispered against his lips.

"Fawad let's run away and get married in the neighboring village." She said pleading.

"I cannot accept you being completely cut off from your family. Despite everything they are still your family. It is essential for our marriage to be valid that your father agrees. I want him to bless our marriage. That is more likely to keep relationships with him harmonious."

"Don't burry your head in the sand. Father do not agree to our marriage."

"I don't want to marry you against his wish. Our time will come I promise you. In time, he will accept me as his son in law. What I can promise you right now: no one can touch you but me."

"Don't you ever leave me. I can't live without you."

"How could I and you are every reason, every hope, and every dream I have ever had. Just breathe and have faith that everything will work out for the best."

"I am afraid of a dark future without you."

"It is the possibility of darkness that makes the day seem so bright. From this day forward you shall not walk alone. My heart will be your shelter and my arms will be your home."

"I have died so many times, but with you I am still alive. Your words bring hope."

"Don't be afraid of tomorrow. When one door of happiness closes, another opens. So keep on trusting and keep on walking. The end will be more glorious than you can imagine."

"But the men father chose for us are coming tomorrow."

"Don't worry. Salman will take care of them."

CHAPTER 10

Salman cut off a tree with his axe, the tree fell down to obstruct the path of the road leading to the farm. The tree intercepted the passage of the carriage drove by the two brothers.

Salman appeared from nowhere. The brothers saw him strong and big like a hulk. They feared him and began to shake uncontrollably.

"What are you doing here?" He demanded.

"We are looking for Misra Bhandari farm." They answered

"There is no farm around here by that name, so just turn around and go back the direction you came."

"We have been here before and we know the place well. The Bhandari farm is five miles from here. Allow our carriage to pass."

"Do as I say or I will cut off your heads." Salman yelled at them.

"No reason to get hostile friend. Misra invited us to get acquainted with his daughters." One of the brothers said.

Salman dragged the two young men by the arms and pulled them out of the carriage. The two brothers hit the ground hard. Salman pressed his feet into their necks, giving them an unbearable pain. The young men felt the bones of their necks pop. Salman pulled them to their feet, gripping them by their necks.

"Now go back to where you came from and never come back again you hear me?" Salman warned with fire blazing from his eyes.

They quickly jumped into the carriage, grabbed the rein and pulled off in haste towards their village.

Fawad and Sonam spent the night in the forest cuddling each other. His arms were the best place to calm her down. She relaxed in his embrace anticipating a happy life together. In the next morning Fawad accompanied Sonam to the house. Salman met him at the main entrance, and both decided to confront Misra.

Misra was in the living room with Mahudri and Ashwaria sitting on a sofa opposite him. As soon as his eyes laid on Sonam he rose from his chair and screamed in her face: "You are bringing shame on the family by disobeying me. You are a bad daughter. You are rebellious."

He put his hand around her throat. "I will be happy to kill you for the shame you brought upon the family by running away."

"Stop torturing her. Hadn't she suffered enough already?" Fawad said taking his hand away from her neck.

Fawad seated Sonam beside her sisters, and stood aside Salman ready to confront Misra.

Misra glanced at Ashwaria and Sonam and said: "Let it not be thought that you reject meeting your future husbands. Chat to them, make them smile, treat them decently. I can't imagine what you find so offensive about them. Don't ruin your chances for real love and real relationship. Cheer up, your future husbands are coming to claim you."

Misra pointed his finger at their rooms and continued: "Now go to your rooms and lock yourselves in. Pray for your future spouses. They need your love now, even if you've never met them."

The girls rose from the sofa and were about to go to their rooms when Salman said: "Stay!"

Misra looked at him amazed.

Salman: "We have been suffering on your account. Stop ruining the lives of your daughters. Your cruelty is enough to drown any heart. Enough torturing us. Enough killing Sharu. You deprived him from Mahudri. You killed him."

Fawad: "I want to see Sharu happy again, but he wants to stay sore. His heart doesn't want to heal, his body died."

Salman: "He doesn't eat, he doesn't sleep. The pain consumed his heart. What has he done to deserve all this pain?"

Fawad: "He smiles so no one sees his silent tears. He has no more tears to shed. Do you hear his cries?"
Tears pooled in Mahudri's eyes and fell harder as pain raps on her chest.

Salman: "What did you do to Sharu, the merciful, the beloved, the compassionate? What did you do to Sharu the farmer, the warrior?" You know who Sharu is? He opens his heart to embrace others. His purpose in life is to serve, to show compassion and the will to serve others."

Fawad: "What are the values you stand for? Boasting about your lineage, money and wealth! We stand for honesty. Kindness, equality, compassion, treating people the way you want to be treated and helping those in need. These traits are the greatest treasures."

Salman: "Yes, and you better embrace them."

Fawad: "We proposed to you earlier but you have rejected us. You have an enormous capacity for lack of compassion."

Misra: "My time is not worth wasting. Salman get out of here and take your ill-mannered brother with you."

Salman: "Not before I tell you something that you don't know. The two spouses you are waiting for will not arrive."

Misra amazed: "I do not understand."

Salman: "I forced them to go back. They ran away like cowards."

Misra yelling hysterically: "You monster! You have crossed all limits. I will kick you out, all of you. You played with the heads of my daughters and seized their hearts, and now you push them to sacrifice the opportunity to have a great marriage!"

Salman glanced at mahudri and said: "Hold your head up. Dry your tears. Sharu is here to comfort your fears."

Salman then glanced at Ashwaria: "Calm your fears. No one can snatch you away from me. Better days are sure to come. The pain will soon be gone."

Fawad: "Sonam my love. What made you think that I will leave you? Hold on tight. I am here for you."

CHAPTER 11

It was a bright sunny morning. The river was glimmering in the sun. Ashwaria ran along the bank of the river laughing and dancing. The water glittered in the sun inviting Ashwaria for a bath. She padded her feet in the cool water. The cool current bubbled over her toes, soothing them. The water felt heavenly. Without any hesitation she took off the garment she had been wearing and dropped it to the shore then stepped into the water. She splashed water onto her face and arms. It felt good. She waded further into the water until it came up almost to her waist and then she ducked under. She began washing her body enjoying the coolness of the water.

As she washed herself in the river, two fishermen came and cast their nets into the water. They stared at Ashwaria with eyes menacing and filled with lust. They eagerly waited for her to come out of the water to rake her body with their devouring eyes. Ashwaria felt extremely embarrassed and was unable to get out of the water.

The two fishermen looked at each other then jumped into the water to retrieve the catch net and catch the fish. Pretending being busy retrieving the net, they approached Ashwaria. Ashwaria became instantly terrified and held her breast with both hands as if trying to protect herself against the upcoming onslaught.

Two hands like a heavy hammer came from behind to grab the shoulders of the fishermen. "Take your nets and cast them somewhere else. Get yourselves out of the water now." Salman yelled at the two fishermen. The fishermen saw a huge hulk staring at them with eyes like flames of fire. They collected themselves and their nets and fled to the other side of the river.

Ashwaria was exhilarated to see Salman, though she tried her best to hide it. He came right on time to save her. He is her beloved and her guardian angel. Salman gave his orders: "Get out of the water now." His voice was a mad growl.

"I am naked."

"What? Are you crazy? You like being watched naked eh?"

"It was just after dawn and no one was here. The fishermen came after I got into the water."

"I will beat the crap out of you."

"Stop talking nonsense and get out of the water. I will be right behind you. Do not watch. Give me your back."

Salman got out of the water and gave her his back. She rose naked from the water, picked up her garment and put it on.

"You know what I am going to do? I will toss you off the nearest cliff."

Before she could answer, He swept her into his arms and carried her across the bank of the river.

"Your madness has got to stop." She said hitting his massive chest with her right hand.

He tightened his grip around her and continued marching forth towards the forest. She knew how to stop him. There are few spots that get him laughing. She kissed his neck, and dove in for a bite. She nibbled at his earlobe. She kept biting his ear and earlobe until he laughed and giggled.

"You can put me down now." She demanded laughing.

He sat on the ground and cradled her in his lap. He searched her face, studied the emotions shining through her eyes. Her silken hair framed his face and fell over his shoulders. He smoothed his fingers over her jaw, her ear, her hair, love shown from his eyes. "I am jealous even of the zephyr which passes over you. I hope you know that deep in your heart." He said angrily.

"Smile. You look cute when you smile. She said staring at his angry features."

"If I didn't care about you, I wouldn't get so angry at the things you do."

"Catch your anger and extinguish it. If you carry a smile on your face, you will feel better. Smile, I tell you."

"I don't feel like smiling."

"Then fake a smile and pretend that you are happy. There is so much to smile about."

"Then say something that would make me smile."

"You are the greatest thing that has ever happened to me. You are the prince I have dreamt of finding ever since I was a little girl. You've been my dream."

He smiled, held her lovingly in his arms, and forgot all about his anger.

It was a sunny day when Sonam and the girls of the farms went with their mothers to the nearby river to fill their clay vessels with water. Sonam and the girls of her age ran along the bank of the river laughing and splashing water on each other. The mothers were busy filling their vessels with water when six bandits from the gang of Agni appeared from behind the trees and chased the girls. They managed to get Sonam and three other girls. They carried them and headed to a wagon hidden behind the trees. The girls were shouting, screaming, and kicking but to no avail. Suddenly an arrow came to pierce the eye of one of the assailants and another came to shatter the neck of another. It was Fawad running after them releasing a volley of arrows causing terror amongst them. When Fawad reached there, the assailants threw the girls to the ground and drew their swords. With his sword and dagger Fawad dealt with the four assailants bravely.

Fawad cut wildly at one man who immediately collapsed. His sword slammed into the face of the second who fell to the ground sunk in blood. The dagger sank deeply into the neck of the third. The fourth fled to the wood but Fawad threw a dagger into his back. The dagger went so deep that it penetrated the assailant's heart.

Fawad escorted the women and the girls to the farm. Sonam walked beside him enjoying his warmth and protection. The women and the girls arrived safely to the farm; and Fawad had something to say to Sonam so he took her to their secret place, a nearby meadow.

Fawad: You are not like the other girls. You should not leave the house or go beyond the courtyard. The wood surrounds the farm from every direction and is infested with bandits and criminals."

Sonam: "They scared the hell out of me. I was about to be kidnapped until you showed up. What do they want of me and the girls?"

Fawad: "How naïve are you? Agni and his gang kidnap women and sell them to landowners to work in their farms as slaves."

Sonam: "O God that would be terrible." She said aghast

Fawad: "The women abducted are beaten into submission and then raped. When they try to escape they are tortured and gang raped."

Sonam threw herself in Fawad's arms crying. "I can't imagine such a thing happening to me."

Fawad: "It could have happened if I was not there. No other man would ever touch you but me, and you have been touched by a stranger to day."

Sonam: "How come! I don't understand."

Fawad. You have been lifted up and carried away by a stranger. He touched your body while carrying you."

Sonam: "It was against my will, I was being kidnapped."

Fawad: "Listen carefully. You are my costliest flower. You bloom for me. No one else would dare inhale your sent but me."

Sonam: "I loved you for some time and I thought that I knew you, but I didn't know that you were so jealous. I love your jealousy anyway because it is a sign of love. I love you my beautiful archer. Recite to me some verses that would ease my heart."

Fawad recited:

"Has the archer shot me, or have your eyes?

"Has the arrow been lanced at me from an enemy, or from your window?

"You are such as would cure the malady of the sick and extinguish the fire of the thirsty."

His sweet voice touched her heart deeply. She surrounded his neck with both arms, and kissed his lips. He wrapped his arms around her waist and kissed her ardently. He whispered in her face: "You are mine. Only mine."

Fawad met Sharu and told him about his encounter with the bandits. Sharu realized that the farm was now surrounded by Agni and Ramesh's people. They were near in the vicinity, and the farm must be ready to defend itself against any attack. The attack was likely to occur soon because Fawad had already killed six of Agni and Ramesh's men.

Sharu: "There is something treacherous going on there, I can smell it. Agni will take revenge and comes after us. The farm is now volatile, so we must be prepared for them. We must make fortifications and train the farmers fighting the bandits."

Fawad: "They do not have weapons to fight with."

Sharu: "We will figure something out. But now we have to buy three good horses to pursue the assailants when they flee back on horseback to their headquarters."

In a nearby horse breeding farm, the three brothers bought high spirited strong horses. Sharu's horse was jet black, Salman's red, and Fawad's white.

CHAPTER 12

Sharu firmly believed that there must be a close watch over the enemy outside the farm. He appointed a watchman to keep an eye on approaching bandits. He thought of building a wooden archer tower to enable Fawad to easily fire his lethal arrows. The tower would also serve as a watching site spotting approaching invaders.

The spacious courtyard of the house was enclosed on only three sides. The front side was left open to overlook the fields. Sharu decided to build a wall and a huge wooden gate to close the front. However, the gate will be left open temporarily for the bandits to get in, then will be closed behind them, and this would make the bandits entrapped within and be vulnerable to the arrows of Fawad and the sword and dagger of Sharu. Salman and the farmers will be dealing with the bandits outside the courtyard.

Sharu orchestrated the whole thing. He chose fifty young farmers to counter attack. He ordered them to make wooden clubs and axes made of wood and stone. The Khan brothers taught them how to fight against potential attacks. They taught them how to draw the knife and parry by dodging and attacking; and how battling with an axe. The most effective strike with an axe is the way they chop wood i.e. they raise and smash.

A watchman came running to say "A gang of the bandits are approaching the farm."

Sharu instructed the villagers to prepare for the battle. He gave his orders to them to take their positions. The bandits are known to lust after young farm women. Sharu ordered the women to lock themselves inside their houses to protect their daughters from the bandits, Misra and his daughters were watching the battle from the balcony. The battle was, vicious, bloody, and not impressive to look at.

The farmers were not familiar with fighting, upon the first encounter with the bandits, they fled and took shelter behind the bushes. But Sharu hastily united them. At Sharu's signal, the farmers charged out of their hiding places, crying, "Death to the bandits." The farmers fought heroically against the invaders.

With their swords and daggers the Khan brothers cut off the heads of the bandits and ripped open their bellies. The arrows of Fawad pierced their eyes and necks. The axe of Salman split their heads and skulls in two. The sword and dagger of Sharu ripped off shoulders, stabbed bellies and rammed into stomachs. There didn't seem to be an end to the fight. It looked as if the entire farm was ablaze.

The bandits then swarmed into the large courtyard willing to get into the house searching for valuable possessions to steal and women to ravish.

Sharu gave orders to Salman to fight with the farmers the invaders outside the courtyard while he and Fawad were to protect the house and deal with the bandits inside the courtyard. When the courtyard became crowded with bandits, Sharu ushered the gateman to close the gate. The gate was closed and the bandits became entrapped inside.

Fawad ran to the tower to fire his arrows from a high altitude as planned. Sharu remained in the courtyard fighting the huge swarm of invaders. The scream of the women which came out from inside the house encouraged the bandits to fight ardently to win the women they wanted.

From the wooden tower Fawad had the advantage of gravity working in his favor. He shot down his arrows to hit the bandits battling with Sharu. There was no escape from Fawad's lethal arrows in such enclosed area surrounded by walls and a closed gate. The arrows came to penetrate the bellies of the bandits and struck their hearts.

The air was sick with Fawad's arrows. There were groans and crying everywhere.

His sword in his right hand, and the dagger in his left, sharu fought like a lion. A bandit stepped towards him but Sharu met him with a quick slash that took his head off. As another moved to attack, Sharu stabbed him in the belly with the dagger. Another came forward, and Sharu stabbed him in the throat and finished him off with another gash to the throat.

Four men rushed to attack. Sharu's sword rushed over their heads stabbing necks, ripping open bellies, chopping heads and tearing shoulders apart.

Fawad ran out of arrows, so he resorted to sword and dagger. He joined the ground assault with Sharu. He used his dagger at very close range, and finished his opponents fiercely and quickly. There had not elapsed more than a little while, before the bandits inside the courtyard were all killed.

Sharu yelled at the gate man to open the gate. The gate was opened and Sharu and Fawad hastened to help Salman and the farmers. Salman and the farmers had already killed fifteen bandits. Sharu and Fawad joined their assault and leaped at the remaining bandits. The three brothers hacked at the bandits in front of them.

The killing became a vicious circle that never ends. And the Khan brothers pushed harder and harder determining to conquer and win. The blood of the dead spread all over the place and the ground became a bloody heap.

Seeing the defeat of his troops, Agni and his brother Ramesh signaled the remaining bandits to retreat. They backed away and flew to the mountains.

Sharu ordered the farmers to dig a deep ditch to bury the dead corps. The khans returned to the courtyard to be sure that the girls and their father were safe.

Mahudri and the girls were in the balcony glancing proudly at their men. Shyam was trembling with fear after he saw the massacre. He hadn't seen a killing before. His violence was only concentrated on women and wine. Misra was also looking proud at the three brothers. They are his men after all. They cultivate the land for him. They collect the profits for him. They protect his land, and his family against invaders. They do that with valor and intrepidity. It was only this thing that annoyed him. They crossed all borders when they wanted his girls to be their wives. "Common men do not marry women of a noble house. Common people were born into a class of people and generally stayed in that class for their entire life. Working hard, and fighting hard, would never change their status." He whispered to himself.

A bandit was still alive. He rose from the ground with a dagger in his hand. He came behind Sharu attempting to kill him. Salman saw him. He drew the axe from his belt and buried the blade between the bandit's eyes. Shyam seeing this sudden kill made him sick. He vomited fermented food mixed with wine. The vomit had a terrible smell defiling the whole place.

Ashwaria stared at Shyam and said: "Why didn't you share with them the fight? I bet you don't know how to handle a sword or a dagger."

Sonam said: "Sword and dagger are made for the brave and not for the drunkards in pubs."

Misra: "Shut up you too. Behave."
Ashwaria: "These are the men we love, the men we long for, and not this coward who shared the fight by watching from the balcony."

Misra couldn't answer back for Ashwaria was right. Neither Shyam who was busy trying to calm down his rebelled stomach was able to utter a single word, though Ashawaria's words penetrated his ear and offended him to the core.

CHAPTER 13

The courtyard looked like a spacious grave. Awful stench announced the presence of the unburied dead. The dead bodies, swollen and disfigured as they were, were lying in heaps on every side. Salman, Fawad and the farmers were busy loading the corpses in wagons to cast them into a large open pit away from the farm.

Dozens of wounded farmers were stretched out on the ground suffering from their wounds. Mahudri and her sisters hurried down to tend the wounds of the farmers. Mahudri was an expert in tending wounds and broken bones. Her sisters were not as good as she was so they worked as her aids.

Mahudry worked slowly among the wounded men. She tended ripped flesh and stressed muscles. She cauterized bleeding, repaired bone, burned away sepsis. At every step the air grew heavier and fouler.

Sharu was sitting in the courtyard on a brick bench. He was bathed in the blood of his victims and the blood of his own wounds and bruises.

His muscles were bunched and stressed. He wanted to close his eyes and sink into the oblivion that will end all his pain.

Mahudri's heart sank to her knee when she saw him drowned in blood. She came with her two sisters; Sonam carrying a bucket of pure water and Ashwaria carrying a basket containing ointments and bandages.

Sharu smiled when he saw Madhuri and his tears rushed to his eyes. She stared at him stricken. "Sharu, why those tears for?

"The mere thought of losing you brings me to tears." He said sadly.

She stared at him with tears in her eyes and smiled regretfully.

"Let me take care of you. Let's clean up a big mess." She said giving him a cup of Datura liquid to drink. He swallowed it in one gulp and before long he felt the pain ease. She soaked a piece of clean towel in the water Sonam was carrying and started wiping out the blood from his body.

"Are you in pain? You are strong. You can handle pain I am sure." She said while drying him slowly starting with his shoulders and back, then moving in front of him.

"Just because I am strong enough to handle pain, doesn't mean I deserve it." She knew that he was talking about pain of separation and not pain from wounds.

Madhuri removed an array of herbs and ointments from the basket Ashwaria was carrying. These she rubbed gently on Sharu's bruises and wounds.

"My muscles are contracted. He pointed to his shoulder's blade."

"It's tight all right." She said running her fingers lightly over his shoulder's blade.

He inhaled deeply as her fingers roamed over his tensed muscles. Her thumbs smoothed over his shoulder blades. With every rake of her finger tips down his back he felt more relaxed. Her slender fingers worked the muscles in his shoulders and smoothed over his shoulder's blade.

"How does it feel now?" She said glancing at his tired eyes.

"Much better I suppose."
She knew that her husband was watching her from the balcony. She didn't care anymore. She had had enough of his torture and abuse, she had had enough of his beating her down all the time. She finally had enough of this agony after being married for two years and having a child in her womb already!

"I see pain in your eyes. Are you happy?" He said observing the dark circles under her eyes.

"I am happy." She said quickly to hide her misery.

He lifted his eyes and glanced at the balcony. He saw her husband watching them.

"I haven't seen your husband in the battle. He didn't fight with us. He was only watching from the balcony. What kind of man is he?"

She didn't reply.

"He should have fought to protect his wife and his own soul."

"He's not a fighting type of guy. He is cut from a different cloth." she said with a wry smile.

"Are you happy?" He said again.

"I suppose so." She said not wanting him to probe further.

"Is he taking care of you?"

He received no answer.

"You deny your own pain to make everyone else comfortable! Talk to me please."

She remained silent.

"Your wounds will heal soon." She said preparing to leave.

"The wound of the heart remains. It is never gone."

"O Sharu please. Forget me, I am with a child now. I am just a memory from the past." Tears rushed to her eyes.

"How could I forget you and you are the air I breathe? I was torn from you but my wound will always remind you that our past is real."

"You are strong, you can forget, you can tolerate the pain."

"Strong people don't put others down. They lift them up. I will stand by you. I can't see you in pain."

She looked up at him shrewdly. "I must go now. My husband is watching us." She left shedding silent tears.

"Now I know you are not happy. Now I know you have been hurting. You are not alone. I will stand by you until I see you whole again." He shouted after her.

Shyam was fuming with anger. He couldn't wait for Mahudri to come to their chamber. It was a total surprise to her to see him meeting her halfway across the courtyard. He struck her with a stick on the posterior, and shouted angrily: "Up to your room."

Sharu was outraged to see this, but he will not confront Shyam now so not to make the situation worse. Now he knew for sure that Madhuri was married to a savage brute. Time will come when he will teach Shyam what brute savagery really is.

In their chamber Shyam slammed the door shut behind them. He shouted in her face: "What were you doing with that man called Sharu? You were practically fucking him before my eyes." He slapped one hand over her mouth and nose and the other against her head. He pushed her to the ground and began his sadistic rape.

She swallowed hard and clenched her fists when he kept punching her face with the rising of his passion. A kind of mantra went through her head. "I will ignore the pain. There is no pain. There is no emotion. I will not scream." She said to herself. She got a punch to the chin. She felt numb. "Die now." She said before losing consciousness and slipped into oblivion.

When she came to her senses, she was looking into Asha's eyes, not quite realizing that she had gone neither to heaven nor hell. Her cheeks burned from Asha having slapped her to make her wake up. Asha was scolding her with tears running down her old wrinkled cheeks. It took a while for Mahudri to get over the shock of being still alive, and Asha to calm her nerves.

CHAPTER 14

Mahudri decided to face Shyam and speak with him about his maltreatment of her. Her life cannot continue like this. She must put a stop to his cruelty and debauchery. Mahudri wanted her father to know the reality about Shyam. Her father was no doubt disconnected with reality. The confrontation with Shyam must be in the presence of her father.

With a bruised face Mahudri rushed to the living room where her father always sit to drink his morning tea. Shyam felt the appalling danger threatening him so he rushed after Mahudri to stop her from meeting her father. But Mahudri was already there sitting beside her father. Shyam sat in an opposite chair ready to defend himself.

Mahudri began her talk: "Father I am being physically and emotionally abused by Shyam. You probably won't believe me but Shyam had been sexually abusing me for the past two years." She cried.

It took Misra a long moment to absorb her words.

Shyam snapped at her: "You are lying. Decent women do not spread the secrets of their marriage. Secrets are a kind of trust, which must be kept. You are betraying a trust. Disclosure is a betrayal of the trust. You should be punished."

Misra: "Mahudri has always been an upfront child. Whenever anything was worrying her, she would come and tell me. She says the truth. My trust in her is unshakeable."

Even though Misra was convinced that Mahudri had been telling the truth a tiny part of him had hoped that she was exaggerating.

"He treats me like a dog. He treats me like a slave. He kicks me. He hits me, he punches me."

"Why do I stay with him if things were so bad?" She added through her tears.

Misra: "I can see the contusions and bruises on your face."

Shyam: "It is every man's right to beat his wife so long as it was to correct her if she did anything to annoy or upset him or refused to obey his orders."

"And what did I do wrong?" Mahudri exclaimed in disgust.

Shyam: "You do not know your status woman. A woman is asked about her husband, a man is asked about his rank."

Madhury: "I also came from an honorable family."

Shyam: I am your husband, I am your Lord. You are nothing but property. You are not even to go elsewhere without my permission. Your job is housekeeping, bearing and rearing children. I will punish you if you say anything disagreeable to me."

Mahudri: "You equate me with property! I have the right to live respectfully and be happy. I have the right not to be tortured."

Shyam: "Only if you do not interfere in my private life."

Mahudri: "What life? The life of debauchery and drunkenness!"

Shyam: "My life is none of your business."

Mahudri: You must know your duty towards me. I am also a human being like you. I have the rights of freedom and respectful life. I am your partner and not a servant. You do not own me."

Shyam: "Don't talk to me like that woman. Do not cross the limits or I will beat the shit out of you."

Mahudri: "A woman is proud of herself just the same as a man would be. Do not insult or belittle me. I expect you to respect me.

Shyam: "Shut up you bitch. I have had enough of your shit."

There was something in Shyam's eyes that scared Misra. He wondered whether Shyam was possessed by an evil spirit.

Shyam seemed impervious to reasoned argument. He launched hurtful attacks on Mahudri and didn't care about her father's feelings.

Shyam raised his hand and slapped her face violently. Blood oozed from her nose and lips. She buried her face in her hand and screamed from pain. She looked at her father to see what his reaction would be.

Misra screamed angrily at Shyam: "How dare you lay a hand on my daughter? She didn't say anything to provoke you. She just stated facts.

Mahudri: "Father I can't live like that. I want a divorce.

Shyam laughing: "If I give you the divorce you will remarry an older man. You are damaged now. No one else will want you."

Misra: "Shut up. I'll kick you out if you couldn't control your temper. I now realized how little I knew you." He said as if apologizing to Mahudri.

Mahudri kept crying from pain. Asha the governess came to calm her down, and attend to her wounds.

Shyam rushed angrily outside the room. Addiction to wine sent him crazy and pushed him to the nearest pub to spend time with his fools.

Misra glanced at his daughter and said regretfully: "He was my choice. A bad choice indeed. Things will turn to your favor. Just have a little patience."

CHAPTER 15

Asha, the governess had a sixteen years old daughter called Amita. Her hair was midnight-black and it flowed over her shoulders. She had honey sweet lips. She had a cheerful character. She was so beautiful that she attracts a lot of attention. She was like raindrops on flowers; like a rainbow at a splashing waterfall; like a full moon shining through a cloudy night sky. When she walks, people turn their heads to focus their attention on her. When Shyam first laid eyes on her, he felt a blood rush in his veins.

One night Shyam came to the farm drunk. He stumbled drunkenly and fell to the ground. He then stood up with difficulty and tried to pull himself together, but he staggered and walked in circles. Amita - Asha's daughter - caught his eyes when heading to the cow barn to provide the animals with fresh forage. Heat rushed into him, and blood rushed into his cock.

He followed her to the barn. No one was there except the two of them. She was bowing providing the cow wooden vessels with forage. Shyam came from behind and grabbed her and pulled her to his chest.

She was about to scream for help, but he put his hand over her mouth. He lifted her and pushed her down on the ground.

He kissed her forcefully bruising her mouth. Amita panicked. Wiggling and kicking she fought against him. He grabbed her dress and yanked it straight up over her head, Seeing her helpless underneath him made his groin stiffen and his heart race. Her body stiffened in fear as he settled above her." Get away from me." She screamed trying her best to break the hold he had on her. "Let me go," she said, squirming under him. The weight of his body kept her pinned to the ground. He took off his lower garment, and gripped her buttocks hard, pulling them forward, then pulled her legs over his shoulders and penetrated her violently. He got up leaving Amitra lying on the ground bleeding and weeping. He left for the house, took a moment to right his clothes and sweep his loosened hair back out of his face, then walked to his chamber as if nothing had happened.

Amita kept lying on the ground crying for hours. Asha her mother became worried. She knew that Amita was out to feed the cows, what kept her late for so long she wondered? Asha went to the barn to see what happened to Asha. She found her crying and bleeding. She understood from the first instant that her daughter was raped.

Asha: "Amita who did that to you?"

Amita weeping ardently: "Master Shyam."

Asha: "His dirt had reached the four corners of the world until it touched my baby." She said in deep anguish and crying bitterly.

Sharu was sitting by the river contemplating the sound of currents lapping at the river's edge. Asha came to the river to fill her clay pot with water. It was the job of Amita to do that, but since the rape Amita was forbidden to go out. Amita's job now was to assist her mother in household tasks. Asha finished filling her pot with water and before lifting it up high over her head, Sharu ushered her politely to sit beside him. She accepted contently. To her Sharu represented valiance and grace.

Sharu: "Asha, tell me about Mahudri. She seems very unhappy?"

Asha: "She is an unhappy woman. She is a miserable ill-fated woman."

Sharu: "Is she in trouble?" He swallowed a lump in his throat.

Asha: "She lives a life of sorrow. She won't eat; she just gives in to her grief, washing away all her hours in tears."

Sharu: "Why?"

Asha: "I can hear them screaming at one another. He hits her. Sometimes I see her face covered in darkened bruises."

Sharu felt his heart pounding in his chest, anger rising in his throat.

Asha: "He is not living with her a normal life as good husbands do. He enjoys rough sex. He hits her if she resists him. Every time she had sex with him she ends up having bruises over a lot of her body. Not just little ones, big swollen painful ones. He rapes her every night."

Sharu was shocked. A sudden wave of disgust washed over him. His stomach rolled upside down. He ran to a distant place and threw up and went on throwing up until he became exhausted. He then went back to Asha and sat beside her not believing what he had just heard from her.

Sharu: "I am sorry Asha. I just couldn't, coundn't..." Words stuck in his throat.

Asha: "I understand my son. I know that you love her, but that what God had decreed – to marry a savage man without compassion."

She stood up and Sharu helped her carry the clay pot over her head. As if she remembered something grievous to say, she paused and stared at Sahru.

"Sharu. "This drunkard brutal savage had raped my daughter Amita in the cow barn a month ago. I concealed the news to protect her from the predators those men watching her with hungry eyes."

Sharu bent down and touched her feet as a sign of respect to this brave wounded mother.

"I will make him suffer. I will make him beg." Sharu said with outrageous anger.

Asha: "Do not take revenge Sharu. You are a noble man. Leave room for God's wrath. For it is written: "Vengeance is Mine, I will repay, says the Lord."

Sharu: "Tell Mahudri I want to see her. She knows where to find me."

CHAPTER 16

Madhuri looked at the mirror and not recognizing who was looking back at her. The right side of her face was bruised and swollen. Her right eye was blackened. What would Sharu say if he saw the damage her husband inflicted on her face? "The bruises had to be hidden behind by a veil. Madhuri covered her head and face by a veil to hide her wounds and went to see Sharu. She went to their favorite place in the woods. She walked amid trees and shrubs searching for Sharu with hesitant eyes. She saw him standing tall and robust, leaning his back on a tree. Signs of grief were shown on his face. She stopped few yards from him. She felt humiliated. Abundant tears came to her eyes. She cast her eyes down ashamed to look in his eyes.

"Are you all right Madhury?" He said in a sharp tone.

"I am fine thank you." She smiled faintly.

"I don't trust your smile. You are lying to me."

"All it takes is a fake smile to hide an injured soul." She turned away her face escaping from his inquisitive looks.

"Look in my eyes and talk to me. What is exactly troubling you?"

She couldn't answer him and remained silent.

"Don't answer me with silence. Say something."

"I came to ease the weariness of my heart." She said at last.

He came closer, and with tender fingers and loving hands removed her veil. His eyes travelled over her face. Her right eye was blackened. Her right cheek was bruised. A burning fire shot straight through him.

"Did someone attack you my lady? Would you ever have told me?

She burst into tears.

"Please stop crying. I can't see you crying."

"What is left to me but to cry out for my fate?" She said sobbing.
He opened his arms to her. She threw herself into his arms and burrowed her face into his neck.

"I think of you all the time. You are what keeps me going." She said basking in the wonderful comfort of his strong protective arms.

A fierce need to protect her flowed through him. He knew in his heart he would die to protect her.

"No one is ever going to harm you again I promise." He said crying.

She took a deep breath and let it out slowly. "I have never stopped loving you. My heart batters by love for you." She said loving his tears and his compassionate embrace.

She raised her head and looked in his tearful eyes. "Let me look at you. I missed your elegant face and lovely smile." She said wiping out his tears with her delicate fingers. A faint smile crossed her face.

"O God, how much I grieve for you. Tell me your story." He said pulling her closer and wrapping his arms tighter around her. She felt more secure and protected.

"Unhappy woman that I am. I am in agony, I am so brutally misused. This is not the first time, but over and over again. When I begged him to stop he didn't listen and when I sought help, no one listened." Her tone was full of bitter hatred. She cried silently.

"He is broke. He married me for my money. My father supports him. I kept company with him through fear of his anger."

"Your words have wrenched my heart." Anger sprang to his eyes.
She lifted his hands to her lips and kissed them. She said while still crying: "God has blessed me with you. You have been my joy, my support. I don't know what I'd do without you being in my life. You are the driving force that helps me survive this blow."

"I will not leave you for your husband to abuse. I would give my life to save you. I will make him pay the price." He said feeling a fire raging in his chest.

"I always prayed: "Dear God, will you ever give me the man of my prayers? Sharu, my love, would the Lord answer my prayers and brings you to me?" Tearful sobs racked her body.

"God will answer your prayers and shower you with His blessings. You will be my wife and the mother of my children."

He kissed her eyes and cheeks. He lifted her hands to his lips and kissed them, wetting them with his tears.

"Rest your head on my heart, and draw from it strength. Feel my arms around you and dream of a better future. Trust in God and believe in His mercy." He said tightening his arms around her.

"Praise be to God, the All-Hearing, the All-Knowing. He is able to do all things. I will wait for you as long as it takes." She said feeling so content and peaceful with his arms around her."

"May the Lord lift up his countenance upon you, and give you peace." He said kissing her hair and placing his chin on the top of her head.

She cradled against his chest savoring the sensations of his kind words and tender touches.

"Let's walk in God's nature and remember the good days. Let's laugh and smile and leave misery behind." He said walking with her arm to arm.

"I will sing for you and you will sing for me. I will ease your soul and you will dilate my heart." He stretched his hands to nature and jumped merrily before her.

He sang:
Storms do not last forever
We will survive the storm together.
You will get through this I am sure.
You are stronger than you know.
Good times are on the way
She sang:
Resurrect me
Make me anew
restore my life
change my fate
Let us be as we once were.
He sang:
You are my favorite joy
yet my endless pain

I will stand by you
Because you are the one that I love
And can't let you go.

Sharu escorted Mahudri to the house. "From now on things will be different. Cast away your fears. I am here for you." He said bidding her farewell.

CHAPTER 17

Shyam found himself broke after Misra deprived him from the monthly allowance. The addiction to wine drove him to madness. He needed the money to go to the pubs and devour the cheap wine he used to drink there.

Madhuri saw him opening her purse trying to find her money. When she saw him steeling like a common thief, anger took hold of her.

"Shyam, put that down at once. Never take money of my purse again. Do you understand?" She snapped at him.

She caught his trembling hand trying to take the money but he snatched his hand from hers and slapped her across the face. Blood oozed out from her nose.

She screamed in his face: "I abhor you and detest your ugly face. My soul is weary of your company. I don't know when God will take your soul away so that I may get rid of you. You married me to use me. Is that was what you were up to?"

"Shut up woman. You should accept everything I do. God gives the husband authority over his wife. Men are superior to women. Women should be subordinate to men." He said with a perfidious smile.

"Does that mean you have the right to steal my money?"

"I do not steal your money, I am just borrowing it."

"Why do you want my money for?

"I love carousing, wine, and comely faces and this I find in brothels. You have heaps of money, so it's okay to take some from you."

He carried off what he could and departed.

Mahudri screamed after him: "Depart and return not here again. You can go to the devil or wherever you choose. Just stay away from me from this time forward."

"You are rough spoken and ill mannered. I will teach you a lesson when I am back." He said departing on shaky legs.

Shyam spent five days moving from one pub to another drinking like a fish. He then returned home seeking hot sex with his wife.

When he saw her, he held her against him tightly. He brought his face down to her neck and kissed her throat. She hated the smell of wine on his breath. She stiffened as he placed his hand on her breast.

"No, stop," she said as she grabbed his hand and pushed him away.

"Don't fight me woman," he said while ripping her sari apart exposing her breasts.

"You bastard." She yelled.

"You bitch." he groaned and punched her face.

"Go ahead and hit me, let father sees the bruises on my face."

"God damn you with your father."

"Dirty son of a bitch. You are a monster, cold blooded monster. Keep away from me."

Her words created the spark that ignited his raging anger.

"I am your master. You must obey me. I will not allow you to treat me like shit. Burn in hell."

He punched her hard on the face. The pain was tremendous as her head hit the wall from the impact of the blow. He kicked her hard in the stomach before beating her to the ground. Mahudri fell to the ground and couldn't breathe for long moments. She rolled to her side and vomited copiously on the wooden ground. Shyam left her thrown on the ground bleeding profusely and went to the guest room to fetch himself a drink.

At that time Sharu was waiting for Misra in the living room to discuss with him farm accounts. Sharu heard a scream, it was Mahudri's scream. Sharu hurried to her room to see what had happened. He saw her covered with blood and curled in a corner of the room. She was crying with a low sound fearing that her weeping might kindle her husband's anger.

Madhuri was sunk in blood. She felt humiliated and extremely embarrassed before Sharu. He was about to gather her in his arms to put her to bed, but she pushed him gently and glanced away hiding from his eyes.

"Don't touch me please so not to get stained. I look awful. I am soaked in blood." She said ashamed and turned aside to lick away the tears.

He said while lifting her off the ground and putting her gently on the bed: "How come and your blood flows in my veins." tearful sobs began to wrack his body.

"Tell them to call Asha please." She said weeping.

He hurried outside the room to call the governess Asha. Asha came hurriedly to attend upon Mahudri and stop the bleeding. Sharu waited outside the room worried to death. His main concern was Mahudri getting better. After an hour Asha came out of the room.

"She lost her baby. She was four months pregnant." Asha said weeping and carrying in her arms a dead pre-matured baby wrapped in a blanket.

Sharu entered the room and kneeled down close beside Mahudri's bed. She was so weak she could barely talk. She cast her eyes down, ashamed to look in his eyes.

"Peace and salutations on her who possesses my soul and my heart. What makes you hide your face from my eyes? Delight of my heart, speak to me." He said with a sad smile mingled with tears.

She said in a weak voice: "I am in pieces. I have been broken. I don't have the strength to carry on. My eyes have become so accustomed to tears that I weep from happiness and from grief."

She looked in his eyes and saw tears gathering in them. She smiled sadly and said lovingly: "There is no one I would ever love the way I love you. Do you still love me as strong as I do?"

"When I to explain the burnings I am undergoing, and the ecstasy of love, neither paper nor pen would remain upon the earth, nor ink, nor a scrap upon which to write. Are not the tears which my eyes have shed up to the present sufficient?"

"Please dispel my grief."

"You whose countenance surpasses in beauty the full moon, and whose face diffuses light over all existing beings, in your presence I enjoy the Garden of Delight."

"Oh! How much I missed your sweet words. How long this separation and deprivation continue?" She said sobbing

"Have no fear my love. I am here right beside you. I am yours." He said kissing her salty tears away.

"Calling me yours is all I want." She said

"I am not despairing of the favor of my Lord; perhaps someday our union may take place. Don't give up. The clouds will clear. No sadness lasts forever. There are brighter days ahead." He said pulling her gently towards him and kissing her forehead and hair.

"You are my rock. You are my fortress. How I love your embrace. My soul rests in your arms. I want to lay on your chest and listen to your heartbeat." She said nestling in his chest.

"Loving you is my life." She said feeling the warmth of his embrace.

"Maybe one day we will reunite and become one soul."

"I just wished you were here so I could tell you how much I need you and how hard every day has been without you. Thank you for staying by my side even though I tried to push you away. Please don't ever leave." She said clinging to him.

"I will never leave you. I will be curled around your heart for the rest of your life. You will get stronger each day I am sure." He said reassuring her.

His deep voice and manly face made her feel safe. How she missed the smell of him. His scent was that of the taste and fragrance of the earth.

"I knew how much you wanted that baby. I'm so sorry about what happened." His weeping words seemed to freeze in his throat.

"I didn't want his child. I could not stop myself from getting pregnant after being raped! I just wanted to die." An obstinate look crept into her eyes.

Silence reigned for long moments.

"Beneath the sounds of your breathing lurks a worry. Speak the hidden words." She said brushing his hair away from his forehead.

"Like a candle I live with a forced smile. I am burning through the fire of separation. I got addicted to my sorrows."

Her tears brimmed over again. "Your remembrance has worn me out. Hold me and let me cry in your arms, please."

She drew him to her and pressed him to her bosom. They wept in each other's arms with a sadness and uninterrupted silence. Their embrace was a kind of relief, but it was also torture because it couldn't take away her torture and couldn't free him from agony.

Her hair was tussled. He pushed the fine long strands against the pillow, and whispered smiling: "I have to go now. I have a job to finish."

"You wouldn't leave me alone in my hour of need, would you?" She said frightened.

"I promise to be your strength whenever you fall weak. I will always be near you taking care of you." He said rising to his feet and heading to the door.

Sharu searched for Shyam. He found him in the guest room drinking wine profusely.

Sharu looked daggers at him. "Why did you hit Mahudri? Why did you kill your child? You were about to kill your wife too!"

"How dare you interfere in my private life like that? You have surpassed all bounds. You are nothing but a servant here. You hear me, a servant." Shyam shouted in Sharu's face.

Sharu: "You have dishonored Mahudri and humiliated her."
Shyam: "I am your master and I command you to get out of here."

"And I command you not to touch her with evil again do you understand?" Sharu said with eyes blazing fire.

In a rush of anger Shyam raised his hand to slap Sharu. Before his hand came up to Sharu's face, Sharu's hand came quicker and slapped Shyami across his face so hard that it was as if his cheek was about to rip open. Sharu gave him another hard slap across the other cheek that took him down to the ground.

Shyam staggered to his feet but he received a severe blow to the abdomen that broke his ribs and sent him dashing to the ground again. Shyami felt a terrible pain and gasped for air.

"It hurts eh! That's what you did to your wife, woman beater. You hit her to make up for your own weaknesses. Woman beater gets beat up too!" Sharu spat on him.

"There are lines not to be crossed with women but you have degraded to the level of beating your wife. You earned her hatred and disgust. It is your bad luck that you hurt a woman that I love. You don't know me. My love for her knows no law, no pity, it dares all things and crashes down all that stands in its path. Hit her again and I will kill you. You hear me dirty, rotten, filthy scoundrel." Sharu shouted outraged.

Misra came rushing to the room and saw Shyam thrown on the ground trying to catch his breath. He understood that Sharu had knocked him down.

Misra shouted at Shyam: "How dare you hit my daughter and makes her bleed? Stop hitting my daughter or I promise you will never see her again."

Shyam couldn't answer Misra. He seemed to be in greatness agony, his lungs ached for air.

Misra continued: "Your brutality has reached to the extent of killing your own son you savage brute."

Misra then looked at Sharu and said angrily: "Although this matter may seem terrible, it is none of your damn business; it is between Shyam and his wife and you must not interfere in their private affairs."

Misra continued reprimanding Sharu: "We people of high rank and dignity do not handle our affairs with servants."

Sharu: "The Khans are not servants. The name Khan means chief or ruler. My ancestors established the world's greatest empire stretching from Turkey to China. Being poor is not a blemish. We Khans eat from the labor of our own hands. We bid to honor and forbid dishonor."

Sharu pointed at Shyam who was rolling on the ground moaning from pain: "Is this the classy man you chose for your daughter? A man who was supposed to make her happy. This man will cause you ruin. All that surrounds him declines and degenerates."

Sharu continued: "You do not care about the good of your daughters; instead, you have surrounded yourself with the mystery of rank and wealth. You brought Mahaudri a debauchee from your class to ruin her life. You are weak. You cannot protect your daughters against life adversaries. Come down to earth and feel people around you or you will die an idle and selfish man."

Misra: "I married my daughter to the man I chose for her. A man of honorable descent. I have had enough of your interference and the interference of your brothers in the life of my daughters. I can't take it anymore. You are not to spend another night in my house ever. I will deprive you from the land I gave to your father. Collect your things and your brothers and leave. Take your mother with you"

Sharu: "Yes we will leave. You have defiled the land when you brought this debauchee here. Wine has robbed him of his understanding. People in his region branded him as a drunkard and a robber. The land is sad; it has stopped producing its crops."

Misra: "Spare me your rubbish talk and just leave."

"I will not leave before Shyam gets his punishment for raping Amita." Sharu said pointing at Shyam curled on the ground.

Misra: "You have cruelly humiliated him. Haven't you had enough?"

Sharu: "Nothing is enough with this arrogant devil. Now listen to me carefully. After we leave, the farm will be more threatened from Agni and his men. Madhuri will not be safe under such circumstances. You are also incapable of guarding her because you blindly side with Shyam against her. Mahudri's safety is my prime concern – more so than my own. She will leave with me. In my mud hut, she will be honored, cherished and respected, until God brings love and justice into her life."

Misra shouted irritated: "How dare you say that? Mahudri is my daughter, and she is married to another man."

Sharu: "What man? This dirt, this dog you brought to her? He said pointing to Shyam. "Mahudri also happened to be the woman I loved even before this dirty scoundrel touched her. Spare me your senseless argument. My decision is final."

Misra: "Your father was loyal to me and…"

Sharu interrupted: "My brothers and I were also loyal to you, but you broke our hearts and denied us the right to love and be loved. You destroyed your daughters, the women we cherished and adored. You ruined them and broke their hearts. We were kind to you but you took our kindness for weakness. The beast in us is sleeping not dead. Beware the fury of a patient man."

Sharu looked at Shyam lying on the ground cringing like a dying fish.

"Can you stand up and fight like a man you coward? You are nothing but a bastard. You are lower than worms. You beat your wife up and humiliate her. You betray her with other women. I am not finished with you yet. I'll teach you a lesson for raping Amita. After that you will never dare to touch another woman in your life." Sharu said kicking Shyam violently in the face.

Sharu left the room and went to see Mahudri. He watched her sleep. He saw tears gathering on her lashes. His love overflowed, and tears dripped down his cheek. He whispered: "Until I see you again, peace be with you."

CHAPTER 18

Sharu knocked on Mahudri's door. She opened the door to him. Her soul revived upon seeing him standing before her smiling kindly.

"You better pack your things. We will leave soon."

"I have already packed them." She said breathing the fresh air of freedom.

"Okay, let's move then." He noticed that she was weak and feeble.
"Lean on me." He said embracing her with his left arm and carrying the bag with his right hand. She put her head on his shoulder and they slowly descended the staircase to the vestibule, and unto the wagon. Sharu's mother was sitting in the back of the wagon. She took from Sharu Mahudri's bag and put it beside her. Mahudri sat beside Sharu on the front seat. Mahudri could feel the mother's compassion without saying a word.

Sharu drove the wagon forth when Misra came rushing down from the house, and ran besides the wagon. Sonam and Ashwaria also came in haste crying because their sister was leaving with Sharu.

Misra yelled at Sharu: "You cannot do that to me. You humiliated my son in law, you disgraced me and now you are abducting my daughter?"

Mahudri replied: "Sharu is not kidnapping me father. I leave with him on my own free will. You ruined my life, you destroyed my body when you married me to this devil."

The wagon stopped at the cow barn. Misra and his daughters reached the barn barely catching their breath. Sharu dismounted and helped Mahudri and his mother out.

Sharu stared at Misra and said pointing to the barn: "There is a party in there would you care to watch?"

"What party?" Misra asked astonished.

The six of them entered the barn to see Shyam with his hands raised over his head and tied to a wooden column. The lower part of his body was naked revealing his buttocks, his legs spread wide.

Salman was standing behind him with a bullwhip. Fawad was there watching.

"His buttocks are enormous like the rump of a cow!" They are white and ripe for flopping." Salman said giggling.

Sharu gave Salman the signal, the whip snapped down across Shyam buttocks. For every stroke Shyam received, chunks of blood flew in every direction. Shyam screamed asking for mercy. But Sharu said aloud: "Salman whip him one hundred lashes."

Salman kept flopping him until his buttocks' flesh was torn apart. Mahudri walked over to him in the presence of all and spat on his face. Shyam then passed out for long moments. After he regained consciousness, Sharu further humiliated him by sitting him backwards on a donkey and led the donkey around the farm. The men threw Shyam with stones and the women spat on his face.

The tour had ended at the cow barn. Misra was standing there boiling with anger. He yelled at Sharu: "You have humiliated me. You have disgraced my son in law."

Sharu responded: "I am a nice person master Mirsa, but if someone is messing with someone I care about, the tougher side you have seen comes out."

Sharu drove the wagon to the village. Salman and Fawad escorted the wagon on horseback. During the trip to the village Mahudri was strained and tensed. Her dark gaze raked over Sharu's profile, detailing every plane, every line. She admired the powerful line of his profile, strong and bold. He radiated character. She saw him brave and wise. And most of all very manly. She couldn't seem to look away from him.

"You felt my frustration and fear and came to my rescue. You eased my heart and restored my dignity" She said gratefully.

"You are my heart. I saved my heart from humiliation and abasement."

"You also restored Amita's honor in front of all people."

"I can get quite nasty when I see oppression in any form."

"I am sorry for all the troubles I caused you."

"Mahudri please. Love means never having to say you're sorry."

"When we were drifted apart, my main concern was about losing you. I'm all right once I realize you're here. I have loved none but you."

"I promise that your life will flow clean, with passion, like fresh water."

"I want us to be lovers again, the way we used to be."

"I haven't stopped loving you since I first saw you. I know there will be much pain, but God will send us His mercy and shower us with His blessings."

She said loving his self-confidence and trust in God's plan: "You know how I see you? Such a lofty, heavenly soul; handsome, graceful and awfully compassionate."

Sharu smiled.

"I love that pretty smile on your face." She said adoring him.

"You are the only reason for it." He said laughing happily.

He sang joyfully:

> God who sits upon the thrown of grace
> Is the God of mercy and peace
> His mercy drops into our hearts
> By night and day

CHAPTER 19

Shyam got mad after Madhuri had left with Sharu. He hated Misra because he surrendered to Sharu and let him take Mahudri with him. He hated the farm and the farmers because he was extremely tortured and humiliated before them. He couldn't escape the angry despised looks following him wherever he went.

Addiction overtook him. He suffered paranoia, hallucinations, muscle cramping and teeth clenching. He needed to use the drug regularly even though he couldn't afford it. Mahudri was not here anymore to steal from her. His father in law was mad at him and deprived him from monthly allowance. The situation was getting worse. He must get the money by any means.

Shyam wanted to know where Misra hides his large sums of money. He followed him secretly almost every day until he knew the hiding place. He followed him to a chamber in which there was a safe having upon its door a closed lock, and over it was a small curtain worked with various kinds of embroidery. Shyam hid behind a couch watching Misra. Misra went to a nearby closet, pulled a key out and opened the safe that was filled with gold and silver, precious stones, pearls and jewels and jacinth. He added plenty of gold coins inside, then closed the safe with the key and put it in the nearby closet. Misra took one last look around the room. Everything was locked and secured. Now he can sleep comfortably without worry.

"This was the place from where I could get money whenever I wanted." Shyam whispered to himself.

In his journeys to the pub Shyam used to steal some of Misra's gold coins and precious stones. Now he knew the hiding place. Now he knew the place of the key. The pub owner and the waiters were amazed to see that Shyan was paying the price of his drinks with pieces of gold and precious stones. The pub owners called one of his waiters and whispered few words in his ear. After a while the brigand Agni and his brother Ramesh entered the pub roaming it with their eyes as if were searching for a table. They headed straight to Shyam's table and saluted him.

Agni: "Hello Mister. The pub is crowded tonight. Do you care if we join you?"

Shyam drunk: "Of course. By all means. Have a seat."

Agni and his brother sat at the table.

Agni: My name is Agni and this is my brother Ramesh. He said pointing to his brother.

Shyam: "Delighted to meet you."

Agni: "Let's get to know each other."

Shyam: "I am Shyan Agrahari. My father owns a large farm fifteen miles away from here. Honorable Misra Bhandari is my father in law. I live with my wife in his farm."

Agni: "You live in the farm where brothers Khan work?"

Shyam: "They don't live there anymore. My father in law kicked them out." Ha Ha Ha. Shyam laughed hysterically.

A wicked smile crossed Agni and Ramesh's faces.
Shyam then called the waiter. The waiter came over to take the order. "Two bottles and glasses for my guests here. Bottle no glass for me. Bring me a woman too."

Wine came and Shyam and his guests drank, laughed, and chatted merrily. Shyam hadn't a clue who were they of course.

After a few moments a woman came and pulled out a seat and sat beside Shyam. His hand left the table top and moved to the inside of her thigh.

Shyan pointed out to the waiter. The waiter came and stood by the table waiting for Shyam to place another order.

"You brought me a beautiful woman this time. You deserve a bonus. That will be two gold pieces for you. And for the lady here seven gold." He pushed the gold pieces across the table.

"This is most generous of you sir." The waiter said smiling. He then lifted his finger up saying: "Upstairs. Second floor on the right."

The waiter moved away from the table heading back to the pub owner.

Shyam glanced at the woman and said laughing: "It never hurt to make a little money on the side." He brought out from his pocket a precious stone and gave it to her. The woman smiled happily examining the stone.

"Go to our room and wait for me there. I will be with you soon." He demanded. The woman rose from her seat and left.

Agni: "You seem very rich. Where do you get all this omit gold from?"

Shyam: "From a treasure locked in a secret room I know my way to it."

A sly smile eased across the lips of Agni and his brother Ramesh.

Shyan rose to his feet and said laughing: "Gentlemen, will you excuse me. There is a woman up there waiting to have sex with me."

He reached the stairs swaying from side to side. He was so drunk that he staggered all the way up. He could see the steps through a drunken haze. He lost his footing and stumbled forward landing on his face. He sat there laughing at himself. The woman came down from the room and helped him to his feet. He leaned heavily on her. They both climbed up the stairs to their room.

Ramesh stared at his brother and said:" People still kill each other for gold these days eh?"

Agni: "Let's get the gold out of there."

Ramesh: "We have an invasion to make. No Khans anymore."

Agni: "It's going to be a picnic. The farm is now easy meat."

CHAPTER 20

Agni, Ramesh and their men attacked the farm. They practiced kidnappings and murders. Fifty farmers were killed, and several others wounded. Forty women kidnapped, raped and taken prisoners. The bandits burned crops, cottages and huts. The massacre continued, becoming increasingly brutal. The remaining farmers and women who managed to escape the assault fled to take shelter under trees and nearby bushes around the vicinity in search of safety. The fight pushed the farm back into deep chaos. The children had no food to eat. Ongoing violence continued to keep people from their homes, Agni burned the farm to the ground making its land not suitable for cultivation; a matter that kept farmers from getting the food they need to survive.

Agni, Ramesh and their gang stormed into the house looking for valuable possessions to plunder. They searched every room and every corner until they found Shyam hiding in his room.

"Well, well, well. Do I see before me, the man who plays with gold and pearls?" Agni said in mockery.

"Where is the treasure you were talking about Mister Shyan?" Ramesh said carrying two big leather bags in his hands.

"What treasure?" Shyan said trembling and still shocked from the sudden assault on the farm.

Ramesh pulled out his knife and slashed Shyan's face. The blade sliced off a large part of his cheek. Shyam screamed in horror. The blood streamed profusely down his temples and cheeks.

Ramesh then put the blade up to his chin. "If you don't talk I am going to cut your throat."

"The treasure is in an adjacent room." Said Shyam trembling all over.

"Show us the way." Ramesh said.

Shyam took them to the treasure. He took the key from the closet and opened the safe revealing heaps of gold and silver, jacinth and other gems, together with oblong emeralds, and large oblong jewels.

Agni and Ramesh stood there with their eyes wide open at finding such a magnificent treasure.

Ramesh opened the two leather bags and loaded them with the gold coins and precious stones.

Shyan had the nerve to make a stupid suggestion.

"We ought to divide the treasure equally between us. After all I guided you to it."

"You were wrong after all. Money do not bring happiness." Ramesh said, and slit Shyan throat with his knife. Shyan fell to the ground sunk in blood and breathed his last.

Agni and Ramesh kept searching the house until they stopped at the cellar. They broke the door open and found Misra and his daughters

Ashwaria and Sonam clinging to their father in horror. Ramesh knocked Misra unconscious with the sword's pommel.

Ramesh pointed to Sonam and said: "This for me."

"And that for me." Said Agni pointing to Ashwaria.

Agni ordered his men to set the house on fire, and cared not leaving an unconscious father alone trapped in a burning house.

The two girls were shoved into a wagon loaded with other women and valuable possessions.

Agni and Ramesh retreated with their men to the mountains leaving the farm set ablaze.

After the bandits departed, the farmers rushed to the burning house and saved Misra who regained consciousness from a certain death.

The abduction of his daughters caused Misra the utmost grief and the most violent vexation. His reason almost departed, and his soul almost quitted his body. He ran to brothers Khan to ask for help. Mahudri and the brothers were sitting on the ground at a round table eating lunch. The mother was standing in a corner preparing tea. Misra rushed in sweating, and barely able to catch his breath. He looked violently agitated. They all rose up out of their places to receive him. Sharu saluted him with the best salutation and with all honor and respect and begged him to sit.

Misra put himself in a respectful posture. He saluted the brothers and kissed the ground before them; after which he stood, hanging down his head in humility.

He said with a broken heart and weeping eye: "May God long prolong your life, and grant you eternal permanence, and may you not cease to subdue those who oppose you, and to be the refuge of those who have recourse to you, and the advocate of those who put their confidence in you."

Mahudri extremely worried: "What happened father? Please speak out."

Sharu: "You have loved us with the utmost love, and you have shown us every kindness. How then could we be happy to quit you, and how could that be when you bestowed benefits and favors upon us?"

Fawad: "Now you are reduced to humility and submission, after your pride and haughtiness!"

Salman: "We did well to him and he corresponded with the reverse, such is the conduct of the wicked."

Sharu: "Although you have broken our hearts, we will not, however, relinquish to serve you. We are all at your disposal and whatsoever you demands we will do it. But tell us your tail, and conceal not from us nothing of your affairs. "

Misra uttered a loud cry and said: "Oh my regret! Oh my disappointment! Agni and his brother Ramesh launched a surprise attack. The farmers were killed, the women were captured and raped. Corpses were left lying all over the ground, huts were left in ashes. The bandits burned the place down. The farm was reduced to ruins. The devils spread fear and panic. A great multitude of the farmers had perished; destruction had entered our dwellings, and drowned us in the sea of death."

Misra continued describing the massacre weeping: "The farm was torched to ashes, men castrated and left to bleed to death, families locked inside burning houses, young girls raped, bones and executed corpses are scattered everywhere."

Mother: "May the curse of God be upon them."

Misra continued weeping: "They rushed into the house and dragged Ashwaria and Sonam forcibly away."

When the brothers heard what Misra had said they were violently enraged, their reason almost departed, and their souls almost quitted their bodies.

"My daughters are the fruit and delight of my heart. They carried them off to doom them to the basest of purposes." Misra said wailing.

"They robbed me off and took all my savings away. I amassed riches and imagined that my enjoyments would continue without failure. But now terror has descended on me, and punish has overtaken me. My heart is between affliction and peril, will you not have compassion on the wealthy who is reduced to poverty?"

The mother glanced at Misra and said: "Whatever thing you have been given is the enjoyment of the present life and its adornment and what is with God is better and more enduring for those who believe and put their trust in their Lord. The wealthy man is not wealthy due to his possessions and his wealth. The wealthy man is wealthy due to his self-content."

The mother then addressed her children saying: "O my sons! Sow good even in an unworthy soil; for good will not be fruitless wherever it is sown. He who does good, receives only good in return. Verily, good, though it remain long buried, none will reap but him who sowed it.

"O my sons! Scatter your good deeds all around, not caring whether they fall on those near or far away, just as the rain never cares where the clouds pour it out, whether on fertile ground or on rocks.

O my sons, by heaven, I desire for you nothing but good and success. I wish your women be your wives and fill the house with your children. Go and fight for them. Return them back. Do not fear death. He whose death is decreed to take place in one land, will not die in any other but that land."

The mother then offered up a prayer in favor of her children for length of life and victory over enemies. She raised her hands to the sky and said aloud: "May God grant you the accomplishments of all your wishes and desires. Therefore, endure with becoming patience what the Lord has decreed."

Sharu: "Soon Agni's power will become as though it never had existed. He will be inevitably overthrown. Brothers, all that happened was by fate and destiny, and for that which is written there is no escape or flight."

Salman: "Its war Sharu, its war. We are going to war." He said with fire sparkling in his eyes.

Fawad: I will make my arrows drunk with blood. My arrows will pierce their eyes and flesh with cruelty and rage. I will tear their flesh to shreds. I will give them death, I will show them ruin."

Sharu: "Salman and Fawad go get the girls then join me at the farm. We will all go back to the farm. We will prepare for war from there."

CHAPTER 21

It was at midnight when Salman and Fawad discovered the house of Agni and Ramesh beneath a rocky cliff. The house had a natural chimney to vent it and a stockade in front. The bandits had been careful to always approach their hideout as not to leave a trail.

Salman and Fawad alighted from the carriage and hid in the bushes surrounding the house. The house was heavily guarded by armed gangs. From their hiding place, Fawad shot his arrows deep into their hearts and into their inward parts. Four of them died where they stood. With his long knife Salman approached from behind, grabbed their heads with his left hand and sliced their throats with his right hand.

Salman and Fawad stormed into the house silently without being heard, searching for Ashwaria and Sonam. They found two adjacent rooms. Salman opened the door of one of them and stood looking at a terrible scene. Agni with two eyes like two burning coals climbing on top of Ashwaria raping her. She was screaming and struggling and trying to push him off her but to no avail.

From his place Salman could see Agni's bare back, and upper buttocks and Ashwaria's bare breasts. Salman's iron hand clawed at Agni's shoulder from behind. Agni turned around to see Salman looking at him with eyes like blazing fire. Salman gave him a blow with his bare hand that took him to the ground.

Aahwaria was utterly ashamed of herself and wished she was dead already before Salman saw her in such terrible situation. Salman looked at Ashwaria in extreme sadness but also in utter anger. He drew his knife and sought to slay Agni, but Agni had turned his back in flight like a terrifying dog with its tail between its legs.

Salman wrapped Ashwaria's naked body in the bed's blanket and carried her to the carriage.

In the other room Ramesh was on top of Sonam claiming his own climax in a series of violent thrusts. Fawad saw the ugly scene; Ramesh's bare back and Ashwaria's bare breasts and thighs. Fawad could feel his blood boil. Ramesh didn't feel a dagger coming from behind to slash his throat from left to right. The blood spurted everywhere staining Ashwaria's face and naked breasts. Fawad pushed the dead man down to the floor.

Fawad stared at Sonam in detestation. She saw his eyes bleeding with tears of agony. At that moment she wished the earth would just open and swallow her up. Fawad was hesitant to touch her and she felt his disgust and repulsion. He wrapped the blanket around her and carried her to the carriage.

Salman drove the carriage in silence to the farm. It was like a funeral journey surrounded by the mourning of two women raped, and the tears of two men feeling their hearts had been stabbed by a treacherous deceitful hand.

The big house of their father Misra was burned to the ground. Salman drove the carriage to the bungalow and left the girls in the care of the mother.

"Under no circumstances will you two ever leave the house. Do you understand?" He screamed at them while descending from the carriage.

After four days however, Ashwaria disappeared from the bungalow without telling the mother where she was going. Salman searched for her in every place until he found her sitting on the bank of the river crying in silence. Salman carried her and threw her into the river as if trying to get rid of her. Sinking down and struggling to breathe, Ashwaria finally reached the bank and crept upon the dirty gravel. Salman kept going back and forth across the bank like a mad man. He gave a great shout that echoed off the surrounding hills and resounded in the valley. He wanted to tear Ashwaria into pieces. How could he love her again and she was defiled by Agni the bandit? He hated her. She was supposed to be his, only his, but now she was public property. Her purity, the thing he loved in her was gone. Her virginity, this costly flower of every girl had been lacerated. Agni the bandit, abducted her, raped her, and kept her for days. He was just like an animal in heat raping her violently without mercy.

An intense feeling of disgust washed over Salman. Ashwaria is an abomination now. He does not want to see her again. He was filled with big shame. She was a defiled woman. She had been belittled, humiliated and denigrated, a shame unto every man. He will kill her and get rid of her disgrace.

He grabbed her to the river and both waded into the shallow water. "Kneel" He commanded. And she knelt down to the water.

"I will kill you here in the river. My sword will drink its fill of your blood. The water will wash off your dirty blood."

"Hurl your sword straight through my skull and make it fast. What use is life for me? Let me die and leave this life I hate. Release me from this unbearable pain. I don't deserve you." She said shaking convulsively.

He raised the sword above his head, and she knew it would soon fall upon her head. Fearing the blow of the sword, she threw herself at him.

She clung to him her arms around his waist. She closed her eyes trying to escape the horrid feeling of the coming blow.

Her sudden move made him hesitate for a moment during which she looked up at him in terror.

She said weeping violently: ""I came under the horrific power of a tyrant with no law to rescue me. The tyrant was the law. Where were you when I was scared and frightened? I needed you to be by my side, but you were not there. Where were you when I was hurt, scarred and bruised? I needed you to heal my wounds, but you were not there."

Tears welled in his eyes. "Shut up dirty tramp and prepare to die." He said trembling all over.

"He almost beat me to death. I kicked, shouted and screamed but I was no match for his strength. There was nothing I could do to stop him. Where were you when I was terrified and left alone to live in fear? I needed you to calm me down but you were not there."

Her words tore at his chest. Waves of weeping racked his body. The sword trembled in his hand, he threw it away and sank on his knees before her. He held her tight in his arms and cried and cried and cried. He couldn't stop crying in her arms. She sobbed violently on his shoulder.

He said shaking uncontrollably: "They hurt you. You have been hurt and I was not there for you. I am here now, stop crying, calm down, please forgive me."

"Who am I not to forgive and I have caused you a lot of pain. I see your pain and counts your tears. I know how to heal your broken heart if you just let me." She said wiping his tears with her fingers.

"I have been always with you even through your greatest fears." He said still shaking in her arms.

"What hurts the most is that I thought I lost you and I am never getting you back." She said feeling his arms around her protecting her from all the adversities life has thrown her way.

"No matter what black cloud is filling your life, there is nothing greater than our love. I love you more than you could ever know. I promise to never leave you, not ever, no matter what you are going through. You are not alone. O Ashwaria, stay safe and be happy. I am here to protect you and take care of you." He said holding her tight as if afraid she might disappear again.

She felt protected in his arms. She felt peace and tranquility. She let her head rest peacefully on his chest and slowly closed her eyes. She could feel a relaxed peaceful sleep coming on.

Sonam also escaped from the bungalow to the wilderness wandering through the mountains and hills. She wanted to rid herself from her disgrace, from the world. It will always hurt to come back and remember what she was once and what she became now. She had been raped, she had been destroyed. She felt frightened and sick to her stomach when she thought of Fawad. What would he think of her now? Would he see her as a victim of the rape? Would he see the rape as an unfortunate incident or would he see it as evidence of her bad character? Who would he blame the assailant or her? Fawad would surely react with anger and blame, and she couldn't stand seeing him hurt. The world became darkness in her face.

Sonam walked through the woods for long hours without food or drink. Though exhaustion overtook her, she proceeded stubbornly until she reached a hill rising high before her. She climbed the hill and stood on the top looking around. Down below she saw a sparkling lake ringed by trees. She descended to the lake. The water lapped at the rocks and the stone surfaces were slippery with moss.

She will get rid of her life. She will drown herself in the lake. She moved deep into the water until it came to her waist. She slipped into a deep spot and the water went over her head. She smiled to herself as she went down to the very bottom of the lake. Here in the bottom, she will rest in peace and surrenders to her fate. But the matter was not that simple. Her mouth opened and the water surged in. Water got into her lungs and set them on fire. Breath was driven from her lungs. She couldn't breathe. She was actually suffocating.

"Fawad, you will come, you would save me like you always did." She whispered inside her heart.

She felt strong arms pulling her up to the surface of the water. His arm around her neck, Fawad swam with his feet and one hand heading for the shore. He put Sonam down carefully on the bank of the lake. He laid her on her face and started putting pressure gently but firmly on the back to get the water out of her lungs. He then turned her over onto her back and pressured her belly to get the water out of her. She started coughing and spluttering.

She regained consciousness after a while. He helped her to sit upright on the shore.

"I was hot on your trail. I knew that you were going to kill yourself."

"I am ashamed to face you, I am a disgrace. I have hated myself, and wished to die. Why did you save me? Why are you keeping me alive?" She said weeping.

"Yes, you are a disgrace. I just can't stand looking at you. Get out of my sight or I will rip your face." He roared and pushed her away from him. She fell and hit her back on the ground.

He felt no pity for her, he rather shouted: "How I suffer! How many griefs I have to suffer because of you? I am in hell."

"And do you suppose it was easy for me? God alone knows what I went through. You hold me accountable for being raped? You are being too hard on me." She said weeping incessantly.

"Fawad, my beloved, I ask your forgiveness for all the hurt I caused you. Forgiveness is required from the generous. Please love me again. Accept me for who I am." A begging hope escaped her lips

Her words infuriated him more. "I would rather die and not love a raped woman. You are now considered tainted property, trodden deeper in the mud. Impossible. Not in my life I would do that. I've washed my hands of you."

He knelt down on the ground before her. "How can I love you again and you have been defiled? He defiled you. He stole your flower. That flower was for me, only me. You understand." He said with a quiver in his voice.

She lifted her tear-stained face and stared into his eyes. She said sobbing:

"You left me to the monster to defile me. You left me with a monster who robbed me of everything precious to me; my honor, my dignity, my purity."

"Stop this nonsense? I was not even in the farm. Your father kicked us out remember!" He said with an expression of furious hate on his face.

"You knew that our territory is surrounded by bandits. If I really meant something to you, you should have kept a watchful eye on me and my sister. You and your brothers are fighters roaming the land without fear."

He felt a pang of guilt strike him in the heart.

"I needed you to be the one to defend me and be on my side, instead I had to live in fear. When my world was crashing down on me, I needed you to be the one I ran to but there was no one to turn to because you were not there."

She stared at him and saw tears beginning to form in his eyes.

"I felt unloved. I needed you to tell me how much you loved me."

His heart thumped inside his chest and his breathing turned harsh. He felt shaken, completely off balance. His entire body trembled. Her words pierced his heart. Tears welled in his eyes.

"My life is worthless if I don't tell you I love you. I will always be yours even if you don't want me." She said through her sobs.

He raised his eyes towards heaven, talking to God: "Lord of the heavens and earth, why didn't you save her for me? How you allowed this to happen? She has been humiliated, broken and abused, and I was not there for her. She is my heart and they have slaughtered my heart."

He wrapped his arms around her and hugged her. He kissed her tired eyes and dry lips." I love you as no other ever could. I will fill your life with whatever makes you happy." He said trembling with love and sadness in her arms.

She burst into tears. Now she felt alive, now she felt home.

He said with a quivering voice: "You have been hurt a lot, and I regret that I was not there for you. I love you and there is no love without forgiveness. Please forgive me because I couldn't save you. Set me free from the torture snapping my heart."

"There is nothing to forgive. I love you Fawad. It is only love that sets us free." She said nestling against him.

He rose and stretched out a hand to help her to her feet, and said:

"Tyrants and murderers might seem invincible for a while, but in the end, they always fall. Arise Sonam, dry your swollen eyes and cast off your garment of pain. No longer shall you be trampled down. Arise Sonam, Fawad is here, Fawad has come."

Ashwaria and Sonam spent terrible nights. They slept together in one bed holding each other. Frequent nightmares reflected their fears and devastated their bodies. They woke up sweating, heart pounding and looking around fearing the rapists might have been hiding somewhere in the room. The nightmares haunted their waking hours and triggered memories that heightened feelings of anxiety. They locked themselves in the room ashamed to meet people and weeping incessantly.

Salman and Fawad heard their weeping and crying, they hurried up to their room to comfort them. When they entered the room, the two girls jumped from the bed and ran to a corner of the room and shouted in one breath: "Don't touch me I can't stand your touch."

Salman and Fawad stared at each other in sorrowful bewilderment. Their hearts melted with sadness. They sat gently on the ground and sang tenderly:

Fawad
Why do you weep?
Why is it you seem so sad?
Won't you show me your smile?
I'd love to see your eyes sparkle again.
I can't wait to see you smile
Fawad is here now
like the solid wall I will protect you

Salman
I do feel your pain
Remind yourself what you once were
Keep your head high rebuild your life
Salman is here to give you strength

Fawad
From the ashes you stand again
Win the race against the wind
Fawad is here now
Like a solid wall I will protect you

Salman
Free yourself from the shackles of the past
Salman is here to set you free
A new life will begin

Ashwaria smiled at Salman. She said through abundant tears: "Bring me joy and hope. Calm my fear. Put away my guilt and make me free."

Salman stood up and stretched his hands to her. She ran to him and threw herself in his chest. He held her tight feeling a sparkle of sadness and anger consuming his whole body. Ashwaria this tender soul, this sacred beauty was raped, abused, and tortured!

Sonam stretched her hands to Fawad and said through her incessant sobs: "Come and hold me, make me feel alive again. Be by my side. Give me strength. Through you and only you, my soul is at peace. You are able to renew me."

Fawad stood up and walked across the room to her. He held her closer. His hard grip reassuring.

"You two haven't been able to eat properly for the past days. Now you are going to eat a good breakfast." Salman said.

"I am not hungry."Ashawaria said.
"I am not hungry either." Sonam said.

Salman: "Fawad, tell them to bring breakfast for the ladies."

The breakfast came on a big tray. They all sat on the ground and each man fed his beloved with his own hand until they were satiated. Fawad and Salman then put the two girls in bed and asked them to try to sleep for they hadn't slept normally for days.

"I will build a hedge around you that no one can break through. Till the end of time you would be inside no heart but mine." Salman said kissing Ashwaria's forehead.

Fawad bent his head, and planted a gentle kiss on Sonam's forehead. She stared at him and smiled sadly. He said calming her fears: "I will hide you in my eyes, but still it will not be enough for me – peace be with you."

Salman and Fawad left the room. Salman turned his face to Fawad and said with a dark and a deadly frown on his face:

"Fawad, we are going to war."

Fawad said: "Yes we are indeed."

CHAPTER 22

Misra and his daughters were homeless now and had to live in the bungalow with the Khan brothers and their mother. The Khan brothers didn't waste time, they worked hard to reconstruct the devastated farm that was burned to the ground. They examined the old foundation of the burned house and found it undamaged. With the help of the farmers they built a new house on the same old foundation. Misra and his daughters moved to the new house.

The burned land became infertile and the brothers had to restore its fertility once again. Abed, their father, taught them how to cultivate the land and keeps it fertile under stressed conditions. Sharu, learned a lot of agricultural practices from his late father. Sharu sat with the farmers and instructed them to limit the size of the fields, so there will always be an adequate fallow period for old fields to regain their fertility. He taught them using legume green manure plants to restore fertility.

Hundreds of goats, cattle and sheep had been stolen and driven away, but their barns, although burned were still standing filled with manure. The manure was added to the soil to supplement the crops with the essential nutrients.

Under the guidance of Sharu, the farmers started building a compost pile by layering organic materials: manures, crop residues, kitchen wastes and weeds. Now the soil had many sources of nutrients and was ready to produce healthy crops.

Salman prepared the soil by ploughing the fields with borrowed oxen. When the soil was prepared, the seed was sown over the fields.

As for Fawad the archer, he was busy hunting deer, elks, birds, fish and rabbits to feed his brothers and Misra and his daughters. The mother prepared the food and made delicious recipes from Fawad's hunting.

Over the days, and months, the farm became exceedingly prosperous. The land restored its fertility, and produced healthy crops. The herds of cattle and sheep became abundant, and the earth smiled again.

Now it is time for revenge. The brothers convened in the Bungalow and fixed the date of the attack. They kept it secret from the farmers until the last moment. As the time for the battle approached, Sharu stood in the middle of the courtyard and called the farmers to gather around him.

He addressed them saying: "You have seen what happened to us at the hands of the bandits. They pillaged and burnt our houses, stole our sheep and cattle, killed our men, kidnapped our women, beat them and raped them. The time has come to take revenge. The Khans are going into battle against Agni and his gang. This battle is the Khans battle and not yours. We will leave you behind to guard the farm with your lives."

Misra and his daughters were watching Sharu's speech from the balcony of the new house. The girls were terrified to see their men going into perdition. Their hearts flipped in their chests. Bitterness twisted inside them as they heard his words. They thought themselves now happy with their men and that time was enough to make them forget and forgive, but their hot blood running in their veins made their hearts feel like volcanoes. Their stubbornness to take revenge after all these months would be more than their mangled hearts could bear. The girls feared they might lose their beloved men in such dangerous encounter.

The girls went to see brothers Khan to dissuade them from engaging in combat with Agni the bandit.

Sharu was in the stable brushing his horse. His back was to Mahudri, and he didn't see her coming. She came from behind and held his abdomen. He smiled and turned to face her. She tried to dissuade him not to battle with Agni.

Mahudri: "Revenge is not worthy of you. If you insist on revenge, you will keep those wounds fresh that would otherwise have healed."

Sharu: "We the Khans believe that injuries are revenged, crimes are avenged. If we are wronged shall we not revenge?"

Mahudri: "Revenge serves no purpose. Revenge and rational thought never come together. Sharu my beloved I fear you may die."

Sharu: "Death is nothing, but to live defeated is to die daily. They killed our father remember?"

Mahudri: Have mercy on me. Think of me left behind devastated."

Sharu: "I would not rest easy until that devil was roasting and screaming in hell."

Mahudri: I thought I could live again with you in peace and happiness but I was wrong."

Sharu: "You know the old saying, 'If the world is unjust, wave a sword, and cut off heads.'"

Mahudri: "I can't believe that you are leaving me. I remember my life without you and I never want to go back to that dreary existence again. You don't know how much I love you. Would I be able to live the rest of my life with you? I knew this would happen. That you would break my heart" She began crying.

Salman was in the courtyard cleaning his horse's hooves. Ashwaria wanted to dissuade him from going to battle.

Ashwaria: "Forgiveness is the virtue of the brave. Forgiveness is the attribute of the strong."

Salman: "I am not good enough person to forgive."

Ashwaria: "God is merciful and forgiving. Forgive your enemies so that God in heaven may forgive you."
Salman: "I don't care if I am in heaven or hell, all I want is to kill him."

Ashwaria: "Our souls may be consumed by pain and misery, but that doesn't mean we have to behave like monsters."
Salman: "I'm no cheek turner. I'll feed him his organs. Perish the universe if I don't get my revenge."
Sonam went to see Fawad who was standing at a wooden feeder feeding his horse hay.

Sonam: "Be forgiving as God is forgiving. Out of God's mercy to us we show mercy to others."

Fawad: "We should forgive our enemies, but not before they are hanged. Have you forgotten what had happened to you?"

Sonam: "No I haven't forgotten. But you need to show mercy, because as much mercy as you show people, that's the mercy you are going to be receiving."

Fawad: "When everything that you know and love is taken from you so harshly, all you can think about is anger, hatred and revenge."

Sonam: "Revenge is never the answer. Life can be beautiful if you look to the future and leave vengeance to God."

Fawad: "I will cut up him in pieces and send his parts into all the areas of Punjab. "

Sonam I fear you may die and we would never be able to live together again."

Fawad: "Death is the natural end of all life. Death is not eternal. Dishonor is."

Sonam: "you've brought so much happiness and joy into my life. You are part of my very being and I could never be complete or whole without you. Tell me I will never again have to return to that terrible existence I knew before I met you!"

Fawad: "Forget the past and think of the bright future we will spend together."

It was a momentum day when the Khan brothers mounted their horses and marched forward towards the gate of the courtyard. Mahudri and her sisters walked beside the horses weeping.

Sharu alighted from his horse and stood anxious before Madhuri. His face gentle and concerned as he saw the signs of fear in her eyes. He brushed her hair back and wiped the tears from her eyes. She put her head on his shoulder seeking support and reassurance.

Salman and Fawad alighted from their horses, and knelt down before their women.

It was the first time that Ashwaria saw Salman's eyes wet with tears. He said with tears overflowing: "Ashwaria my love. Why don't you understand? Why you torture me? I live with a heart on fire. I can't live like that. I want inner peace to enjoy my life with you. There is no way out but to pour his blood out by the force of the sword. His blood will clean you from the uncleanliness he infected your body with."

Ashwaria: "I am sorry darling for all the agony I caused you. But the love I carry for you is too enormous that I can't imagine a life without you."

Salman: "I will come back, and that is not a broken promise. I will kill him for us to start anew."

She knelt before him and embraced him. They wept sad tears. Their tears mingled and mixed.

Sonam cupped Fawad's face in her hands, while tears coursed down her cheeks. "I feel like I'm waiting for something that isn't going to happen." She said bitterly.

Fawad: "O please don't say that. I will be back for you."

Sonam: "Crazy how much you meant to me but how worthless I was to you."

Fawad: "I love you better than I love my own sole. Our love is like the divine love of God for man.

Sonam: "The burden of you leaving me is getting too heavy. You leaving me is like chains wrapped around my veins."

Fawad: "I will unravel the chains and set you free. I'll be strong for you. I will be your hero."

He rose to his feet and held her close. "I know how hard it must be on you. But you must understand that I carry your heart with me anywhere I go. You are my fate. You are my world". He said reassuring her.

Sonam: "All right. Go get it done, but come back in one piece."

Fawad: "Thank you for the understanding. Thank you for loving me for who I am. I promise you love with no worries. There shall be no more regrets, I will be your peace. So keep calm and be at peace."

Mahudri said addressing her sisters: "Now I understand. The best way to love our men is not to change them, but instead, help them achieve their greatest tasks. Let things flow naturally forward in whatever way they like. I feel the anger in their bones. I see the blood which is to quench their thirst. I don't want the fire in them be quenched. I see them victorious. I see them come back to give us the life we hope for. Fear can hold us back from our reaching our greatest heights. Do not grieve them, they are not going away. They are in our hearts and there they will stay. Do not grieve them for they are not alone. God is with them guiding their every step."

The Khans mounted their horses and spurred them forward toward the mountains where Agni and his bandits reside.

CHAPTER 23

Brothers Khan put spurs to their horses and made them leap like stern lions. The wind whistled under the hoofs of their horses. They covered 12 miles a day. At the end of each day they built a camp.

A word came to Agni that the brothers Khans were seen in the vicinity of his territory. He summoned his aid and ordered him: "Collect your men quickly. Let's take the heads of these dogs."

The mounted bandits and those on foot gathered around Agni who was surprised to see that his enemy was just three knights without farmers to help them during the battle.

Sharu seeing Agni and his men descending the opposing cliff to the valley where the encounter was due to happen alighted from his horse and ushered his brothers to do the same. He said while drawing lines on the ground: "A frontal attack could be effective. Fawad and I will attack the front. The aim is to wear down the enemy to the point of collapse through continuous losses in personnel and weapons. As a skilled archer,

Fawad's arrows would have a distinctive effect during the combat. His arrows would surely cause heavy losses to the front. My sword would cut off heads and stab bellies fast and quick. We will exhaust their front line and before they have had the opportunity to re- organize themselves, Salman will come from behind to smash them. Salman will not attack before he receives my signal. It will be when I use my spear in fighting."

"Now let's do our prayers to God asking for help." Sharu said facing the Kiblah. Salman and Fawad stood behind Sharu who led the prayers. After they finished praying, With tears of reverence in his eyes Sharu raised his hands to the sky and invoked God's help in these words:

"O our Lord, You in Whom the one in need and distress seeks refuge, we complain to You of our weakness. Our state among them is as You see. Our number is few and our weapons are limited. They have ravished our land, abducted our women and killed our men. O You Whose kingdom cannot be pillaged, Give us shelter by Your rank which is never overcome! O Succor of the poor, we trust in You! O Cave of the weak, we rely on You! O our Lord, pour patience down on us, and make our foothold firm, and help us against the evildoers. O Lord, help us against these mischievous people. O our Lord, make us not a trial for the unjust people and deliver us by Your mercy from the wrongdoers. Ameen."

Salman and Fawad repeated after him: "Ameen."

Brothers Khan then mounted their horses and shouted at Agni in the valley below.

Sharu: "We will reduce your dwellings to ruins, so that the owl and the raven should cry in it."

Salman: "We will burn you with our fire. We will dart at you our destructive sparks."

Fawad: "I wear the warrior's bow. When I struck out, I do not repeat the blow. A nightmare is about to begin."

Sharu: "We are the strongest. The touch of oppression affects us not, and the drawing of the sword does not disquiet us; we fear not the sting of the most envenomed foe; we own submission to none, far or near."

Salman: "We will scatter the heads of your men one after the next. Murderers, put on the garment of death the Khans are coming."

Brothers Khan then gave their horses their strength. They made them leap like lions, striking terror with their proud snorting. Salman raced south until he was in a position behind the bandits. He waited for Sharu's signal to attack.

When Sharu and Fawad reached the bandits they dismounted from their horses and rushed on them. Agni and the bandits thought that two persons were easy meat, but they didn't know the heavy artillery of Fawad.

Fawad was the finest archer in all Punjab. His arrows came winging from all directions so that it was difficult to determine where Fawad was positioned. Fawad began releasing his arrows. So powerful and accurate were his shots that he could hit any bandit he chose within more than a thousand feet. The bandits were amazed to see that Fawad could grab two or three arrows at a time, and fire them in rapid succession. He even fired his lethal arrows while running or jumping.

The arrows strongly penetrated the necks, bellies and breasts of the bandits, killing many. In the meantime Sharu pressed forward fighting with his sword and hooked dagger. He drew his dagger and sank the blade deep into his opponents' bellies. He cut off their limbs, hands and feet. He waved his sword over their necks. The sharp blade took off their necks in clean cuts. Their skulls went bouncing against the bloodstained earth.

The spear which was hidden in Sharu's garment is now got to hand. Salman show his brother fighting with the spear, so he rushed like a tiding wave from behind and attacked the bandit's rear.

Salman dealt powerful strokes, wielding his axe with both arms, he brought it down with all his force upon his opponent's heads thus splitting them in two. Salman fought with shield and axe and sword. He plunged the sword into their bellies. Because he loved challenges, he fought with extreme madness.

Salman was so skilled he could throw two spears together using both hands, or catch a bandit spear and send it back. He passed through the rear line to the front and helped to dislodge the bandits from their position.

Desperate fury made the Khan brothers insensitive to pain. They felt a rising tide drum in their ears, the pounding of their hearts as they quickened in berserk fury. Nothing could stop them.

The Khans fought with swords, axes, spears, daggers and arrows. Sharu led them forward. You would have seen men falling, brains flying and bowels lying on the ground. Fawad unleashed volley after volley of arrows into them. The brothers strove as best they could, slaughtering bodies and cutting men down. The victims made horrible groaning as their brains were being battered in, and the ground seethed with their blood. Great was the slaughter; the soil ran red with dead corpses and blood for the ravenous birds to feed. Many souls were driven out of their bodies and the living had to jump over the dead.

The bandits kept on withdrawing while Sharu and his brothers advanced and fought as hell with arrow, sword and spear.

Agni spotted Sharu and intended to strike him with his sword but Sharu struck him first and knocked him down to the ground. Sharu continued giving him blow after blow with his sword caring not to kill him now. Agni was terribly wounded but was still breathing.

The remaining bandits seeing the fall of their leader and the heavy casualties they suffered, escaped to the mountains leaving behind their dead, and wagons loaded with food and water.

Sharu shouted at Fawad: "Tie the devil up good and put him in a sac"

Fawad tied Agni's hands together behind his back with a rope, put him in a sack and tied the top then shoved him in a wagon.

The victorious Sharu and Salman mounted their horses and raced back to the farm. Fawad however, tied his horse to the wagon where Agni was shoved in and drove slowly back to the farm.

In the farm courtyard, Agni was taken out of the sack and forced to his knees, his hands tied behind his back. His shirt was in shreds. He was bleeding so excessively that his clothes dyed red. There remained not a joint of any of his limbs but in it is a broken bone, dislocated joint or a deep bruise.

Mirsa and his daughters and the farmers gathered around Agni the disfigured. Sharu spoke to the gathering: "This is the man who killed our father, our men, and kidnapped our women and raped them. This is the man who terrified the territory and plundered our homes. This is the man who showed no mercy to people but rather oppressed and humiliated them. God is merciful and loves mercy. God is just and loves justice. He wants to see His mercy and justice spread to all over his earthly kingdom, and this man and his gang spread mischief in the land.

"Mercy means compassion and forgiveness. Justice means fairness and equity. He who does not show mercy to others will not be shown mercy by God. This man has defiled the land, shed blood and killed people to make unjust gain. He practiced extortion and committed robbery, he oppressed the poor denying them justice. Evildoers get the deaths they deserve. I will destine him for the sword, and he will bow down to the slaughter.

"Today is the day of vengeance. My sword will drink its fill of his blood. My sword will cut off his head. I will put an end to his uncleanness. I will use my sword to realize justice."

Agni sank back exhausted. Fawad straightened him up and pointed to Salman. The sword of Salman came down on Agni tearing his right arm from its socket. Salman glanced at Sharu who dragged his sword and with a blow cut off his head. The head fell rolling in the dust. Salman picked the head off the dust and turned it to Fawad to aim at. Fawad took an arrow from the bow on his back. He pointed the arrow toward the head and fired. The arrow penetrated the right eye. Fawad shot a second arrow that penetrated the left eye.

Sharu stared at Salman and said: "The head and the body are not to be buried. Scatter his body remains over the mountains, making him an example to the stationary and the passer-by. Give his carcasses to the birds of the sky and the beasts of the earth."

Salman put Agni's remains in a wagon and drove away.

Madhuri was watching Sharu from a distance. She was amazed to see this charming compassionate man has turned into a lion getting revenge on Angi the bandit. He and his brothers launched a terrible war against Agni and his gang and won. The three of them without any support were able to defeat Agni and his troops. Man can give his woman love and compassion but also protection which makes her live in peace and tranquility. Love and peace is that makes life worth living.

Mahudri felt an ardent longing to hold him and feels the warm of his protecting arms. His look was stern and sad. She wished he would smile again. That kind smile that always captured her heart. She walked to him in hesitating steps. He was leaning on his sword with his right arm. She held him tenderly and he held her with his left arm. She lifted her head to him and said smiling: "Relax. You need a rest, a long rest."

Her voice was like a divine melody landed on his ear from the sky.

"Yes, I am tired, I need a long rest." He said smiling in her face.

His compassionate smile squeezed her heart. He still can smile even in such horrible circumstances just to appease her fright.

"I love you. You are the love of my life."

His smile got bigger. He kissed the top of her hair, her eyes and nose and lips.

"Mahudri my love," he said loving her beautiful face. "The agony we all went through hurt so deep it cuts like a knife. The battle with the bandits was fierce and bloody, and we have killed a lot of them. I hate being away from you, but I yearn for privacy and solitude. I will go to the mountain to relax and wash my spirit clean. Going to the mountains is going home. I will stay in the mountain hut until spring. Please try to understand."

Mahudri: Your home is here beside me and not somewhere else. You are every reason, every hope, and every dream I have ever had. But I understand. You can go wherever you want. In the end you will always come back to those who are really meant for you."

"Yes darling. True love has the habit of coming back." He said loving her beautiful countenance.

Salman finished the task Sharu gave him – to get rid of Agni's corps. He felt an ardent longing to see Ashwaria. His emotions erupted and the heat inside his body boiled over. He searched for Ashwaria and found her at the pond their usual place.

He terrified her by coming up behind her shouting aloud: "Ashwaria." She turned around terrifying. "You big fat monster." She said hitting his massive shoulders with her tiny hands. He didn't stop at that. He carried her and threw her into the pond. He stood watching her struggling to come out of the water, and his laughter lashed out in the clear air. She came out of the water willing to tear his face off. But his boyish giggling laughter made her laugh. He opened his arms to her and she threw herself into them thanking God for his safe return.

Sonam knew where to find Fawad. She will find him herding sheep on the hill. He was actually there singing with his lyre a soft song.

The sky is bright.
The air is fresh.
The green grass grows all around
My heart is delighted.

"Good morning handsome. I love you." She said running to him. He held her tightly happy to have her in his arms. They sat on the grass and she rested her head on his lap. "If you only knew how much I missed you." She said kissing his hand.

"Tell me about you since I have been gone." He said moving his fingers tenderly over her hair, brushing her forehead with his lips.

Life felt like a nightmare since you left. My heart felt like it was being weighed down with a thousand stones."

"I am here now darling. Now you are safe in my arms, now you can live in my body."

She sat straight but remained squarely on his lap. She looked intensely in his eyes and said: "What did you do in the battle? Tell me every detail."

"I repressed rebels and defeated enemies." He said not wanting to probe further.

"That is not enough. Say more." She said persistently.

"Help me forget the bloodshed and body parts scattered. Time heals all wounds. But not this one. Not yet. My wounds run too deep for the healing. Turn my sorrows into love. Come to my arms and make me feel alive again."

His pain tortured her heart. "I am sorry dear. Come to my arms. Let me kiss your wounds away." She said holding him with tears overflowing.

CHAPTER 24

It was winter when Sharu went to the wilderness. It was the first time snow falls in Punjab. The snow kissed the trees and covered them up with a white quilt. The trees were bare and the wind blew cold.

He walked for days heading to the mountain. He climbed up the mountain and resigned in the mud cottage. He walked around searching for edible wild plants to eat. He lived on wild garlic grass, clover, bamboo shoots and the tasty leaves of curled dock. He stayed weeks in the cottage meditating. Meditation awakened his heart and mind. He moved closer to his thoughts and emotions. He relaxed more and more into the open dimension of his being.

Sharu felt a strong yearning to God. He felt grateful to him. God is beneficent and merciful. He has covered him and his brothers with victory and enabled them to combat evil and spread peace in the land.

He supplicated to his Lord:

"O God, purify me and makes me whiter than snow. Makes me to hear gladness and joy. Creates in me a clean heart, and renew a right spirit in my inward parts. Do not cast me away from Your face and give me the joy of Your salvation.

"My Lord, make the farm secure, and grant us out of our wives and our offspring that which cheers our eyes.

"O Lord, forgive me and my brothers and admit us to Your mercy, for You are the best of the merciful."

The winter with its cold had passed away, and the spring had come with many kinds of beautiful flowers. Bees were busy moving from one flower to another in search of honey. The river formed the most enchanting cascade, and the singing of the birds was truly delightful. The yellow flowers of mustard fluttered in the breeze. The earth wore a green garment, and light graced the tree tops. Spring transformed the wood into a paradise.

He longed for Mahudri. Now he was ready to go back. It was delightful to walk under the beautiful canopies of spring bloom. The green plants pleased his eyes. Heavy dew covered everything with small beads of moisture. There was nothing, no voice, only silence. The only silence was the occasional drip of dew on the wet leaves that covered the ground all around him.

He walked down the mountain and reached the fields. He walked through the corn-fields. He saw friendly cows chewing the cud. He scratched their foreheads and patted on their backs.

The tall trees rose out from the mist as he walked towards the farm. Salman and Fawad were on horseback guarding the farm against any intrusion that might happen during their brother's absence. They spotted Sharu coming from afar. Fawad rode fast to the farm to inform Mahudri about Sharu's arrival. Salman spurred his horse in the direction of his brother. Salman embraced Sharu and welcomed him back, showering tears upon his arrival. Fawad on horseback emerged from the mist after a short while. He cordially embraced his big brother and welcomed him to the farm.

"Mahudri is hot on my trail." Fawad said pointing at the footpath leading to the farm.

Salman gave a wink to Fawad, and they both disappeared in a wink of light.

Sharu beheld a radiant form rise among the trees. Mahudri looked radiant like the moon at the full. Sharu was enchanted by her appearance. His heart raced when he saw her. He stood in silence, focusing all his will on reaching out to her.

She spotted him standing there contemplating her with a compassionate smile drawn on his face. She walked up to him in small steps with a radiant smile on her face. The happiness she felt at that moment made her tears flow. She ran up to embrace him, but she stopped a few steps before him to contemplate him further. He was a joy to watch. She loved the way he looked. His adorable smile made him look more beautiful with his thick beard and long hair. She inhaled his strong male scent. His scent was that of a ripe earth, a thing that refreshed her soul.

She kept standing there looking at him with tears rolling down her face. "Sharu my love. Life without you was unbearable. Bidding you farewell is like bidding life farewell. In your presence I enjoy the Garden of Delight." She said with a tremulous voice.

"There you are perfuming the world with your scent. If God gave the sun a day off, people would know how you shine all the time." He said opening his arms for her.

She threw herself into his arms crying. "I love you so much; you are all I have. I was so alone without you. Life looked like a barren desert."

Sharu: "I never loved anyone as I loved you. Beyond you nothing I could see. I do not enjoy the sight of the world but by your sight."

Mahudri: "I missed your lovely words. Have you missed me too?"

Sharu: "I will make up for all the years I was supposed to be kissing you." He said kissing her hair, eyes and lips.

Mahudri: "You have been in the mountains for long, are you okay now?"

Sharu: I am better than I was. I am waiting for my real life to begin with you. I want to live the rest of my life with you. I want you to be the mother of my children. Are you ready to marry a man who has never stopped loving you?" He said lifting her hands to his lips kissing them.

They walked over to a wooden log and sat on it.
"Tell me about your seclusion in the mountain." She said eagerly wanting to know the output of his experience.

"In my seclusion God was my refuge. It was an invitation to rest my heart in what was true. I saw days cloudy and gray. I saw days bright and sunny. I watched sunrise and thought of you. Always you. I remembered your pain, your agony that wounded your heart and left a scar on my soul. In my refuge I saw no pain, no suffering, just love. I saw you so pure and peaceful as a butterfly finding at last its missing wings. I came to realize that you are only mine, that it would be only me that you will be spending the rest of your life."

She looked plainly into his eyes and said worriedly: "I have been thinking a great deal while you were in the mountain. You have sacrificed a lot for me and my family. We have been a load over your shoulders. You defended us by sword and dagger. You restored peace and established justice. You never ceased to care for us. Do you accept marrying a woman that had been humiliated and trodden under foot?"

His body quaked. He went down to his knees and took her hands in his. She saw abundant tears sparkling in his eyes. She knelt before him.

"It was my heart that had been trodden. You are my heart, my today, my tomorrow. You are in my thoughts. You are in my prayers. I can't think of a day without you. Please smile. Make my heart smile again." He said crying incessantly.

"I had been a beautiful orchard with delicious fruits ripe for you to take, but the devil turned me into a barren garden with no fruits." She said weeping ardently.

"Don't cry my love. We together will turn the barren land into pools of water and the parched earth into springs. We together will open up rivers on the barren lands, and fountains in the midst of the valleys."

"I suffered immensely. He had ruined my life. I lived in total darkness."

"Stars can't shine without darkness."

"He broke down my walls."

"I'll rebuild the walls and add windows to let sunshine in."

"Do you accept the blemish he tarnished me with? He left me broken with scars, bruises and flaws."

"The eye does not see a flaw if the heart loved the heart. Try to forget. It's over now darling."

"But in my heart it was so real."

"Don't be the girl who fell. Be the girl who got up. What happened to you was a blessing. A lesson learned."

"I lost the will to live. I thank God that He has sent you back to me. Forsake me not."

"Who am I that I should forsake you? I accept you for the person that you are. I love you so much it hurts."

He kissed her lips tenderly and wiped out her tears with his fingers. He held her close, and she felt home. His embrace was her real home.

Mahudri realized from his encouraging words that she may be temporarily harassed by all kinds of trials. But this is not accident. Life is not without meaning. God knows what's going on. He's weaving the fabric in her life. He brings good out of bad. There's something more important than her pain, it's what she had learned from that pain. She must never lose heart. She must believe in a brighter future with the man she loved. She must forget and love with all her heart. She may never have that chance again.

"Come live in my heart and forget your pain." He said stretching his hand to her.

Hand in hand, fingers entwined, they made their way back to the house

CHAPTER 25

The earth spread out a green carpet. The daises opened up and the world blossomed. The sun had risen on the farm dispelling the clouds of grief. The fragrant zephyr of union had blown and revived the sad hearts. The beauty of delight had appeared with perfumes, and the drums of victory over evil and the settling of peace have been beaten in the province.

It was a spectacular day when the three brothers stood before Misra respectfully asking again for his daughters hand in marriage. Although Misra was extremely happy to see that the brothers still wanted to marry his daughters after what happened to them, he was also enormously embarrassed.

When he heard their persistent proposal, he fell to his knees crying ardently. He touched their feet respectfully. Sharu tried to help him to his feet, but he said: "No my son let me talk begging on my knees. I got a lot to say."

Misra was overcome by emotions and kept crying for a long time. When the sobbing had subsided enough for him to talk he said: "Although our custom prohibits widow marriage, Sharu insists on marrying Mahudri. Although rape deter men from marrying women abused, Salman and Fawad still insist on marrying Ashwaria and Sonam. I can't face men of honor like you with such disgrace."

Misra continued still crying: "My perspective about suitable husbands for my daughters was totally wrong. I should have found good husbands for my daughters but I ran after the false pretense that they should marry men of high status and I neglected the fact that man is not by his status or wealth but by his character, integrity, courage and the ability to affect those around him positively, and you my sons have done all that.

"I forced Madhuri to marry the wrong person. I ruined her life. My girls were abducted and abused and you brought them back safe. I deprived them from their right to love and be happy, and you gave them love and made them smile again. The land was burned, the house was demolished, and you rebuilt the house, and cultivated the land. Evil and death overshadowed the land, but you repelled evil and spread peace over the land. How could I repay you? I always wished to have sons but I only had girls. Do you accept being my sons…my only sons?"

"We are honored to be your sons. Let's not talk about the past. Let's kick out errors and enjoy a bright future." Sharu said getting Misra to his feet.

The three brothers decided to tie the knot together on the same day. The girls were ceremoniously decorated, and marriage ceremony was conducted. The weddings were filled with ritual and celebration that continued for several days. The three couples shared the same house and the love they carried for each other made them get on so well.

The home that was bare of beauty and joy, became a blossoming garden. The Khans planted the seeds of multiplying and propagation that yielded heaven's richest gifts - beautiful boys and girls, brothers and sisters, living together in sweet accord with the music of an unbroken song of holy peace.

After few years from marriage we see Sharu carrying his son on his shoulders and pulling his daughter with his right hand. Mahudri walking beside him carrying a newly born baby.

At the pond we see Salman reprimanding his son while his daughter standing crying at a distance. Ashwaria was standing laughing wholeheartedly at Salman and holding on to his shoulders for support.

Salman was angrily shouting at his son: "Haven't I told you several times before not to throw your sister in the pool?"

Salman then looked angrily at Ashwaria who was still bursting into laughter. She understood from his look that he was going to throw her in the pool as well. So she ran away laughing. He ran after her pretending that he was going to throw her in the pool, but he stopped after a moment bursting into a loud laugh.

Fawad was with the sheep playing his lyre and singing his favorite song:

> I saw her walking in coquetry
> My heart said tik tik tik

Sonam danced and sang with her two sons:

> He knocked on my heart tak tak tak
> My heart beats faster tik tik tik

Their joy and happiness culminated in a big dance festival. Mahudri, Ashwaria and Sonam with the young women of the farms in the background danced like luminous glowing pearls. The music was exquisite and the words were soft and tender. The girls sang while dancing:

> Happiness has come
> Sadness has gone
> The earth has smiled

> The flowers have bloomed
> The green has spread
> The birds have sang
> The soft wind has blown
> The branches have danced
> Peace returned to the land

Brother Khans danced with their women for a while then separated and danced together the song of war:

They have defiled our honor and violated our dignity

> They took our lives away
> They didn't know that
> The touch of oppression affects us not
> The drawing of the sword frightens us not
> They didn't know that
> We own submission to none far or near
> We are not afraid of thunder or lightning
> We followed them to the edge of the earth
> We flew like eagles and stood like giants
> We were like daring lions

We brought peace and made frowned faces smile
Now we have it all to live for